# BONUS BOOK

## THE STONE SERIES: EXTRAS

BONUS CHAPTERS, MUSIC PLAYLISTS,
& RECIPES FROM YOUR FAVORITE CHARACTERS

*USA TODAY* BESTSELLING AUTHOR

# DAKOTA WILLINK

# BONUS BOOK

THE STONE SERIES

DAKOTA WILLINK

# BONUS CHAPTERS

ETCHED IN STONE
YULETIDE TEMPTATIONS
MEETING STONE

# ETCHED IN STONE

# THE STONE SERIES 3.5

## ALEXANDER & KRYSTINA'S HONEYMOON

**A lot can happen on a remote island when nobody is looking…**

Alexander promised me a dream honeymoon. He gave me that and so much more. We escaped to a secluded, untouched island far from the bustling world. Surrounded by white sand, turquoise waters, and lush palms, we embarked on a journey of love and unbridled discovery. My enigmatic husband was as ruthless as he was tender. He had complete control, making my skin burn and my body ache. On the last night at our tropical paradise, the atmosphere was charged with anticipation.
I was at the mercy of his every whim, and his obsession knew no bounds. I belonged to him.

# CHAPTER 1

*Krystina*

Alexander and I walked along the Caribbean shoreline's powdery, soft white sand. It stretched for miles, beckoning me to sink my toes into its warmth. Palm trees swayed lazily in the salty sea breeze, their slender trunks and canopy of vibrant green fronds reaching forward. The water gently lapped against the shore, producing a soothing melody that harmonized with the rustling of palms and the distant calls of seagulls.

"It's so beautiful here. It makes me not want to go home," I murmured. The stunning landscape seemed to be plucked right from a postcard. Alexander had said the island was named Enchanted Isle for its hypnotizing beauty. I couldn't help but wonder how he had discovered the remote location for our honeymoon spot. "You never told me. How did you find this place?"

"I can't give away all my secrets, angel. That would spoil things for the future," Alexander replied and flashed me an enigmatic smile. My new husband's sapphire eyes seemed impossibly bluer against the reflection of the crystal turquoise waters.

We continued to walk silently, both content to enjoy the island's serenity. Throughout our trip, we had made the rounds to a few more populated islands, such as Grand Cayman and the lush volcanic island of St. Lucia. However, we always returned to the peacefulness only Enchanted Isle could offer. There wasn't a soul in sight, nor did we expect there to be since nobody lived here. This little romantic haven was too small to be developed. The rocky outcrop and coral formations added diversity to the scenery, but it made docking any sizable boat close to the shoreline near impossible.

I looked past the colorful reefs to see *The Lucy* proudly floating on the glimmering surface of the water. The dinghy we took to shore was just ahead, nestled in the sand. Today was our last day here, and once we pushed the little boat into the water and made our way back to the grandeur of *The Lucy*, it would signal the end of our honeymoon.

We had taken the long way, traveling all the way from Montauk Marina to the Caribbean. Unfortunately, our jobs didn't allow for a lengthy trip back home. The return would be much shorter. Once we pulled up anchor, we'd go north to Fort Lauderdale. From there, Alexander and I would catch a private plane back to New York and leave the hired crew to navigate *The Lucy* back to Lake Montauk.

Even though I knew our life in New York awaited us, I

wasn't ready to go back. It had been three weeks of bliss with my new husband. Our trusted crew members had navigated the boat, sticking mainly to the control room and their private quarters, ensuring our paths would only cross if one went looking for the other. This allowed Alexander and me privacy aboard the expansive yacht. Explosive, lust-filled nights with me bound and at the mercy of Alexander's every desire were followed by seemingly endless days on shore.

"Let's stay on the beach a little longer," I suggested. "Maybe we can catch the sunset from the beach."

"I don't want to tender back to *The Lucy* in the dark, Krystina. It's not safe. We can stay for a bit but can't be on the beach when it dips below the horizon. You'll have to see the sunset from the main deck."

"Fair enough. I'm just not in a hurry for this to end. I couldn't have imagined a more perfect honeymoon. Thank you, Alex."

He didn't respond, but his longing expression shared my sentiments. He didn't want our time here to end, either.

Determined to make the most of our last evening on the beach, I increased my pace to close the distance to the dinghy. Once at the small boat, I reached inside and pulled out the beach blanket I had tucked into one of the small storage compartments.

"Alex, can you grab the cooler? I packed it while it was inside the boat, and the weight of the ice might be too heavy for me to lift. I thought we might have a little celebration on our last night here. I grabbed a Bluetooth speaker as well in case we wanted music."

When he didn't respond, I glanced over my shoulder to see him staring at me with one eyebrow raised. The lid to the cooler was already open, and in his hands were the two fluted glasses and the bottle of champagne I'd packed earlier that morning.

"Planned ahead, did you?" His tone was severe, ensuring I'd note his displeasure. Still, when I looked past the firm set to his jaw, there was no denying the dark desire brewing in his eyes.

"Perhaps," I replied coyly and turned my back to him to spread the blanket over the sand. I planned to strip out of my coverup until I was wearing nothing but my black thong bikini, but my intentions were interrupted when I felt Alexander's arm snake around my waist. He pulled me roughly to him, and my back pressed against his solid torso as his lips moved to my ear.

"Did you forget that I'm in charge? That I'm the one who plans and makes the decisions for you?" he said with a certain level of gruffness that was only heard when he used his dominant voice.

There was a time in our relationship when I would have challenged his stern reminder, but I was a fast learner. This was all part of the game—and the reward for playing was always worth it.

"I haven't forgotten," I said quietly, waiting for his lead.

He pushed his hips slightly forward until I could feel his hardening length.

"You want to celebrate, do you? Don't move."

He stepped away, leaving me with a delicious tightening in my core. Alexander had set only one rule for our honeymoon. He was to be in complete control at all times, and that included any sort of planning. I'd broken his rule by putting together this romantic interlude on the beach without his knowledge. I was in trouble.

Serious trouble.

And I couldn't wait to be punished.

Like the good submissive I had promised to be on our honeymoon, I lowered my head. My toes curled in the silky white sand as I anxiously waited for what would come next. I heard a cork popping from behind me, followed by the sound of pouring liquid. Alexander didn't speak but simply moved around to the front of me. His unbuttoned white linen shirt billowed in the tropical breeze, giving me a full view of his bronzed chest. I ached to touch him, but I remained still.

Reaching up with one hand, he cupped my neck and brushed his thumb along my cheek. His other hand brought a champagne-filled flute to my lips.

"Drink," he ordered. He tilted it slowly, allowing me time to swallow the bubbly liquid until the glass was empty. When he pulled it away, I languidly swiped my tongue over my bottom lip in a deliberate show of seduction.

"Are you planning to get me drunk so you can take advantage of me?" I whispered teasingly.

Alexander's eyes darkened, and he tossed the flute onto the sand.

"It's not taking advantage when the person in question is already mine for the taking. And make no mistake, Mrs. Stone. You *are* mine."

Slipping a finger under the thin strap of my coverup,

he slid it down my arms until it pooled at my feet. After a few quick tugs on the strings at my neck, back, and hips, the scraps of material that made up my bathing suit fell to the blanket. Desire thundered through my veins. The uninhibited feeling of standing naked outdoors was unparalleled. My body flushed, and wetness gathered at the apex of my thighs, wondering what he would do next.

*Would he take me right here on the beach? On the blanket, perhaps. Or maybe from behind, with me bent over the boat's edge.*

The idea caused the devil on my shoulder to twirl in a happy dance.

Alexander's hands went down to my ass, kneading my bare cheeks as he pulled me closer to him. His erection pressed hard against my belly, nearly stabbing a hole through his shorts. His need was hot. So hot. I wanted to slip my hands inside his waistband and give him pleasure, but he held me tight, and there wasn't room for me to maneuver a hand between us.

Instead, I reached up and laced my fingers into his dark waves. He lowered his head to mine, coaxing my lips apart until our tongues danced in perfect harmony.

"I need to punish you for disobeying me, angel," he growled into my mouth.

"Hmmm…"

"I want you bent over the edge of the boat." He stepped back, and I moved into the vulnerable position without hesitation. I shivered when I felt his hand skim up my thigh. My breath quickened, and despite the balmy air, goosebumps prickled over my skin when he spoke again. "Hang on tight to the side of the boat and spread your legs. I'll be giving you five strikes. The first will be for disobeying my orders and planning something without my consent."

I sucked in a breath and braced myself. We'd been here before, and I knew it would only be a matter of seconds before I felt the sting of his palm.

He gripped my hip securely with one hand and widened his stance. Then he let his hand fly. The crashing of the ocean waves drowned out the sound of the slap, but it was no less felt. My body vibrated, humming in the most exquisite way as I awaited my remaining spankings.

"Three more, one for each of the fluted glasses and the bottle of champagne." Alexander fired off the next three smacks in rapid succession, alternating cheeks and making each slap harder than the last. Then he leaned close to my ear and whispered, "The fifth spanking is just for my pleasure. I love seeing your ass red from my palm."

But the fifth didn't come—at least not right away.

I released a quiet hiss when I felt his finger trace the seam of my ass. Endorphins, arousal, and adrenaline created a heady feeling that was all-encompassing. He lingered over my tightest hole for a moment before continuing his exploration, stopping only to cup my mound and feel how wet I was for him. He growled his approval.

"You never disappoint me, angel."

Without warning, he shoved two fingers inside me while delivering the final smack to my ass. I hadn't been ready for it, and my body lurched forward. I quickly widened my stance to keep from toppling into the boat.

Using my new position to his advantage, Alexander

plunged his fingers in further, and I cried out from the pleasure. He played my body like a fiddle until I thought my strings would snap from the tension. His treatment was rough, demanding, and unyielding.

And I loved it.

He leaned forward until his mouth was close to my ear.

"You want to come?"

"Yes," I breathed.

I expected him to intensify his motions, but he abruptly pulled out of me instead. All the air released from my lungs in a frustrated *whoosh*.

"Later, angel," he informed coolly. "And only if you follow my every instruction."

*Shit.*

I hated when he refused me an orgasm, but I knew I'd follow his every command until I got my release. I might not get what I wanted now, but he wouldn't deny me forever.

"Okay," I whispered, desperately ignoring the ache between my legs.

"Okay, what?" he demanded.

"Okay, sir." My breath hitched as the breeze skittered over my bare nipples.

"Very good. Now, we need to start heading back to *The Lucy*. It will be dark before long," Alexander said matter-of-factly. It was as if he were oblivious to my desperate panting.

*The bastard.*

I looked past him to see our world had transformed into a mesmerizing canvas of vibrant colors. The sun had dipped closer to the horizon, painting the sky with a breathtaking spectacle of orange, pink, and purple. The lower the sun got, the deeper the shades would become.

"You're right," I agreed reluctantly, my voice throaty and breathless.

Alexander lifted my naked body, cradling me to his chest by hooking his arms behind my back and knees, and lowered me into the dinghy. Releasing me, he turned to collect my discarded bathing suit and coverup.

"Put this back on," he said and handed me the bits of material. "It will be off again soon enough, but the crew on *The Lucy* doesn't deserve a show in the meantime."

"How soon will I get to take it off again?" I teased as I tied the bathing suit strings at my neck.

Alexander's heated sapphire blues narrowed on me as he dug his feet into the sand and pushed the boat into the water.

"Not soon enough."

# CHAPTER 2

*Alexander*

The salty breeze tugged at my hair as I carefully secured the sleek dinghy to the side of *The Lucy*. I fastened a sturdy painter line to the bow, ensuring it was taught enough to accommodate the sea's ever-changing moods. In a sense, the rope was a lifeline connecting the small vessel to its mothership. It was a ritual I'd performed countless times but never gave it less care than the last. Knots were my forte after all—as Krystina could attest— and I tied each one with the finesse of an artist.

Once I felt satisfied the small craft was secure, I turned and offered my hand to Krystina. The sun was low in the sky, its red streaks blazing across the horizon and basking my wife in an orange glow as she stepped onto *The Lucy's* polished deck.

*My wife.*

I wondered if I would ever get used to that.

My angel was officially mine.

Now and forever. And while that may sound infinite, no measure of time with Krystina would ever be enough.

Leaning down, I pressed a kiss to the top of her head. "I need to talk to the crew for a moment, and then I'm going to see about getting us something to eat."

"I hadn't even realized we skipped dinner, Alex. If you'll give me a minute to get some proper clothes on, I can—"

"Clothes won't be necessary," I interjected. "Just head down to our bedroom. I'll get a light dinner together and bring it there. And angel—I want you naked and kneeling when I get there."

"But—"

I raised a hand to silence her and shook my head ever so slightly. I didn't need to say anything. My expression was enough for her to know I would not be challenged. The protest fell from her lips as understanding settled over her.

I raised my hand to lightly brush her cheek with the backs of my fingers, skimming my thumb along her jawline.

"Your trust is intoxicating. Go and wait for me. I won't be long, angel."

Without another word, I turned to walk toward the helm with a confident stride, crossing the main deck to where I expected the crew to be. When they came into view, Isaac Davis, the crew captain, looked up when he heard my approach.

"Mr. Stone," he said with a short nod.

"Good evening, Isaac. Are you prepared to pull up anchor?"

"Yes, sir. Rough seas are forecasted for the overnight, and I didn't know if you wanted to try to navigate that. Just waiting on your orders."

I pressed my lips together into a tight line. The ocean waters in this part of the world were always unpredictable this time of year.

"Hurricane?"

"No, sir. Just a small tropical storm to the north that will bring considerable chop."

"I'd like to avoid that. Let's bring her around to the island's south side and anchor there for the night. Hopefully, the land will provide a bit of protection from the harshest of the waves. We can begin the trip back to port in the morning when your crew is ready."

"Very well, Mr. Stone." Turning toward the other two crew members, Isaac addressed them in a firm and authoritative voice. "Start the engines!"

Each subsequent command was spoken with precision and clarity. I was pleased to see their movements well-coordinated and synchronized, a testament to their experience and training. After starting the powerful engines that lay hidden beneath the sleek exterior deck, *The Lucy* began to move with the refined elegance the luxury yacht was known for.

"Steer to starboard," Isaac directed. The helmsman adjusted the wheel, and the yacht responded gracefully. I nodded my approval, trusting Krystina and I would be in good hands on the overnight.

Leaving them to it, I walked across the large open deck. Away from the harsh city lights, the stars shone brightly, illuminating the sky like shimmering diamonds. They reflected on the large double glass doors that led to the salon. After sliding the door closed behind me, I moved to the small galley kitchen and opened the modest refrigerator. I was pleased to see Isaac had restocked everything precisely as I'd requested, making it easy for me to assemble a quick, no-cook meal.

I arranged tomatoes, red onion, olives, green peppers, and cucumbers on a platter. I topped it with cubed feta and a seasoned oil and vinegar dressing to complete the traditional Greek salad. Once that was finished, I prepared another opulent platter of cheese, nuts, and a medley of fruits. Hearty crackers paired with velvety hummus and creamy tzatziki completed the simple meal. Even Vivian, my invaluable housekeeper and cook, would be impressed. It may not have been one of her seven-course spreads, but it would suffice.

I placed both platters on a serving tray, grabbed two glasses and a chilled bottle of Louis Jadot Le Montrachet Grand Cru 2016, and went to the master suite.

When I opened the doors to the bedroom, my breath immediately caught in my throat. I froze, completely mesmerized by the stunning woman kneeling near the foot of the bed. With her arms behind her back and her knees apart, she defined the meaning of perfection. Desire gripped me, and I suppressed a groan.

She glanced up at me curiously, then quickly lowered her head in submission. In the brief moment that our eyes met, I saw the silent invitation. She knew her body belonged to me.

Tearing my eyes away from her delicate and creamy skin, I set the tray of food down on the small dinette in the corner and lit the candles already strategically placed around the room. The candlelight cast shadows that seemed to amplify the silent passion in the air, whispering promises of what would come.

Walking over to the settee, I picked up a coil of black nylon rope that draped over the back. Tonight, on the last night of our honeymoon, Krystina would be rendered helpless. I would own her, demanding her submission until every one of my desires was satiated.

I took off my shirt and moved to stand behind her. My eyes ran down the length of her flawless spine and settled on the curvature of her impeccable ass. A vision of those luscious hips opened to me flooded my brain.

*Not yet.*

I was nothing if not patient, and I knew the reward would be worth the wait. Squatting down behind her, I looped the rope around her wrist and went to work.

In the dimly lit room, sexual tension hung heavy in the air. The sensation of Krystina's wrists in my grip, the feeling of her vulnerability and trust, was intoxicating. It fueled the primal desire that coursed through my veins. I watched as her hands, delicate and graceful, succumbed to my binding. As my fingers brushed against her skin, a shiver coursed through her body, a thrilling response to the impending restraint. There was a moment of resistance, a flicker of uncertainty, before she willingly yielded to the erotic tension enveloping us.

It was a dance of dominance and submission, a sensual interplay of power and trust that left us both breathless. I gripped her neck and angled her head back to look at me. Her eyes filled with a mix of anticipation and surrender. She held my gaze, and at that moment, we were bound not just by restraints but by an unspoken understanding of the exquisite pleasure that lay ahead.

Once her bindings were secure, I stood and moved to the table and retrieved the tray of food and drink.

I selected a succulent, ripe strawberry, bringing the bright crimson to her lips. With deliberate slowness, she parted her lips to accept the offering. Her teeth grazed it delicately with a hint of a knowing smile playing on her mouth.

This went on for the next thirty minutes. Each morsel I offered her, each shared bite, became an intimate exchange of desire and pleasure until I thought I might combust. I wanted her more than I ever wanted her before. It was an unexplainable need of epic proportions. I was desperate to be inside her. To feel her velvet heat.

Pushing the tray of food to the side, I reached up with both hands and brushed the pads of my thumbs over her nipples. My touch caused them to harden into erect peaks instantly. She sucked in a tiny breath, followed by an exhale of desperation. I pinched, twisting each nipple between my thumbs and forefingers, relishing the weight of her bare breasts in my hands. When she moaned, any willpower I had to put things off any longer was thrown to the wayside.

I lowered my head and took a ridged peak into my mouth. She gasped in pleasure as I sucked and rolled her around my tongue. She tilted her head back, inviting me to take more, and I silently thanked all that was divine for gifting me this woman.

Moving up to claim her mouth, I pushed my tongue past her waiting lips and devoured her. She moaned, the vibration of her lips sending an electric shock straight to my groin. Our kiss was a dance of passion, conveying emotions that went beyond any spoken words. It was a revelation of our deepest desires.

I worked my way down her neck, savoring the feel of her pulse hammering beneath her skin as I breathed in her scent. She smelled like coconut-kissed vanilla.

"God, Krystina. The things you make me want to do to you…"

I nipped up her neck to her earlobe. She lolled her head to the side and allowed me better access. I wrapped my arms around her and pulled her body tighter against me. She sighed her appreciation, and I crushed my mouth against hers again.

Lifting her, I wrapped those glorious legs around my waist. The heat of her sex pressed against the ridges of my abdomen. She pushed forward, grinding against me, telling me her need was hot. I could have buried my cock in her right then—to drive into her like the wild animal she made me. But she deserved more than that tonight. My wife merited worshipping.

I set her down on the edge of the bed covered in silver and blue satin. I kissed down her body, over her shoulders, breasts, and thighs, savoring the delicious taste of her skin.

I spread her legs apart and pressed my cheek against

her inner thigh. Her exposed lips were lush, pink, and inviting.

"Oh, angel."

My face hovered over her glistening sex, and I blew softly until she began to pant. I couldn't wait any longer. I had to taste her. I swiped my tongue over her clit. Her breath hitched, and she cried out. It was all the encouragement I needed to bury my face in her soaking wet heat.

I reached up and took hold of her breasts, gratified to feel her nipples still pebbled from arousal. I twisted and pulled at the taut peaks. The pulsing in her clit signaled she was already near release, but I kept her on edge and didn't allow her to come. Her back arched as I circled and teased, deliberately driving her to madness.

Her breath was ragged when she looked down at me, eyes wild and full of passion. Her cheeks were flushed, and her gaze was desperate.

I pushed her backward onto the bed. Her bound hands forced her back into an arch, elevating her breasts. I shoved her legs up roughly and spread her wide. Then I devoured her like a starving man who would never get his fill.

It wasn't long before she cried out. Her juices, the sweetest of all nectars, coated my tongue and lips as I suckled every drop of her release. I felt a tremble course down her legs and smiled in satisfaction.

"I've only just begun, angel."

Taking advantage of her lithe state, I removed the rest of my clothing. My cock sprung free, happy to be released.

Climbing back onto the bed, I flipped her onto her stomach and straddled her hips. With experienced fingers, I quickly untied the rope binding her arms together. Once completely unraveled, I slid off the bed and fashioned new knots. These would be to secure her ankles to the bed posts.

Once she was secure, I looked to see if she showed any level of discomfort. Her head was angled to the side with her lips parted slightly. But her eyes—those pools of chocolate brown—were dark with want. She knew how defenseless she was in this position. Lying face down, her ass and pussy were vulnerable to my every desire.

"I'm going to bury my cock inside you. Deep. You'll feel every inch of me." I paused and slid a finger over her puckered rear. "Everywhere."

Her response was a carnal moan that was music to my ears. I skimmed my hand down to part her wet slit. One finger. Two fingers. I slowly and deliberately stretched her, preparing her for my invasion. She was more than ready for me.

I positioned myself at her waiting entrance. Gripping her hips, I speared her opening, easily sliding to the hilt. Her breath caught, and her mouth went slack as she absorbed each stab of pleasure. I moved hard and fast, in and out, working her into a desperate frenzy.

"Alex, make me come. Please! I need to come around you!"

I loved when she begged. Something about the way the word please sounded on her lips made me wild with lust.

I kissed the back of her neck and shoulders, then pulled

up her hips until she was on her hands and knees. With her ankles still secured to the bed posts, her thighs were forced further apart. Every intimate part of her was open and more exposed to me than ever. She exhaled and closed her eyes. I groaned and pushed forward until the tip of my cock was pressing against her very core.

"Oh!" she gasped in shock.

I knew how much she liked it this way—deep from behind, with my cock hitting every internal pleasure point. White-hot pleasure rocketed through my veins as the walls of her vagina constricted to adjust to me. She wrapped me in heat, pulsing with desire.

"Come for me, Krystina."

I pulled back slowly, then drove home again. And again.

"Alex!" she screamed out. Her body writhed with pleasure, her climax vibrating around my cock. But I didn't stop. I wanted more—to take and give all I could.

She was like a goddess with her head thrown back in passion—her opulent chestnut curls a wild mane around her head and her lush breasts bouncing as I thrust into her. I gave her bottom a light smack.

"Yes!" she screamed out. "Again!"

*Holy fuck. This woman.*

"My angel likes it rough. You need to be dominated. You crave it."

I smacked her again, this time harder than the last. I pounded into her, spanking her repeatedly until her ass was bright red and my palm stung. Krystina clawed at the sheets, rocking and moaning as I possessed her. She was wild with need, and I knew she'd take anything I had to offer.

Without breaking our connection, I reached over to the nightstand and retrieved a butt plug and bottle of lube. Krystina watched me, her eyes wide with trepidation. However, we'd been here before, and she trusted me. The ultimate pleasure was only a breath away as long as she relaxed her body enough to accept it.

And that she did.

With ample lube, the plug slid in without a hint of resistance until all I could see was the jeweled end. Once it was in place, her pussy clenched impossibly tighter around my cock.

"Fuuuuck," I moaned.

Then I began to move again. I pounded into her with a savagery like never before—dominating her. Owning her. She was mine, and I was hers.

For all of eternity.

I took us higher and higher until I felt her stiffen. Reaching under her, I pinched her clit just hard enough to heighten her orgasm. When her climax rocketed through her body, she screamed.

"Ahhh, Alex!"

Her sex tightened like a vice around me, and I knew I would soon follow her.

I gripped her hips and slammed into her.

"Krystina, I'm right there!" I hissed through clenched teeth.

"Let me feel it deep. Please, Alex!"

*Please.*

Her spectacular cry was enough to send me over the

edge. My mind went blank before a bright awareness spread through me. I plunged deep and held the position, allowing my seed to erupt into the intimate recesses of her body.

My connection to the extraordinary woman beneath me was complete.

# CHAPTER 3

*Krystina*

I lay there staring out the portside window, waiting to catch my breath. The moon cast a silvery glow on the water. The gentle waves seem to serenade us, their melody so enchanting I could easily drift off. Every inch of me was splendidly numb, languid, and sexually satiated.

"Oh no, Mrs. Stone. I'm not done with you yet," Alexander murmured into my ear. His body lay sprawled over my backside, with most of his weight balancing on his right side so he didn't crush me. "But first, you need to eat more. I got distracted before we could finish our meal."

As if on cue, my stomach gave a little rumble. That hour-long sex-a-thon had clearly worked off what I had eaten just a short time ago.

He shifted down my body, trailing light kisses over

every inch of heated skin until he came to a stop at my ankles. Deft fingers released my bound ankles before moving back up. He tapped me on the hip, signaling I should flip over. Once I was flat on my back, he repeated his handiwork. This time, he bound my wrists to the headboard.

"I can't eat if my hands are tied up," I pointed out.

"I will feed you."

*Of course, he would. How silly of me.*

I felt the corners of my mouth tilt up in a knowing smile, anxious to find out what else my husband had in store for me.

After my wrists were anchored to the posts, he shifted my body until I was propped upright against the pillows, allowing a bit of slack in the rope so I was more comfortable. Then, his hands were on my face, angling my head so he could crash his mouth onto mine.

I liquefied beneath the demand of his warm lips. The kiss was hard, hungry, hot, and lethal as his tongue danced to an erotic tune.

Almost abruptly, he pulled away, climbed from the bed, and returned with the food tray. Setting it to one side, he positioned himself before me, lifting my legs until they draped over his thighs and disappeared behind his back. I glanced down to see his heavy cock resting on the bed between us. I swallowed the burn in my throat, the need to feel him on my tongue overwhelming.

Alexander plucked a seedless green olive from the tray and brought it to my lips. His sapphire blue eyes darkened as he pushed the briny tree fruit into my mouth. While I chewed, his free hand traveled down my throat, traced a path between my breasts, and stopped only after reaching my drenched sex. He slid a finger along the slit. My walls pulsated in anticipation, the clenching adding pressure to the butt plug that was still in place.

He continued to tease various pleasure points on my body while feeding me an assortment of olives, cheeses, and tomatoes. His fingers were magic, sparking heightened awareness everywhere he touched. He caressed and explored until my body was quaking with unparalleled need.

But he wouldn't give in to my pleas for release. I began to lose track of time. At some point, he fashioned clamps to my nipples. The hard points protruded through the tiny vises, vulnerable and sensitive to the slightest touch. When he leaned forward to flick his tongue over an erect peak, I nearly bucked off the bed.

"Alex, please!"

I felt the curve of his smile on the side of my breast, and I wanted to scream. My need and desire were so hot it was near agony. So when he finally curled his fingers inside me, my orgasm was instantaneous.

"That's it, angel. Come for me," Alexander demanded in a gravely tone.

Air stole from my lungs, freezing me in place as the intense swell surged through me. It rose faster and hotter until I thought I was going to explode. Stars dotted my vision when Alexander plunged a third finger inside me, flexing mercilessly to prolong my orgasm. Wave after wave of pleasure rocketed through me.

"Oh, God." I could barely breathe the words as I rocked

my hips, milking his fingers until the tremors began to subside. A delicious tingling extended to the tips of my every extremity.

Once I'd come down from the intense high, he removed his fingers from my body and shifted closer until we were mere inches apart. He brought his gaze to my lips, then raised his hand to place the fingers that were slick with my juices to my lips.

"Lick them clean," he ordered.

Meeting his eyes, a magnetic pull intensified our connection as I parted my lips enough for him to push his fingers into my mouth. My tangy flavor, combined with his salty release from earlier, coated my tongue, reminding me of the intensity of our connection.

*Oh, shit. This is hot.*

I swiped over and around each digit in a sensual dance, eager to please him. He stared intently at me while I suckled as if he were memorizing my every move. Sometimes, his eyes would fix on mine, only to shift down to stare at my breasts a moment later. I loved how he looked at me. His gaze said he appreciated what he saw and that my body pleased him—that I pleased him. The low growl that emanated from him was only a confirmation of what I could see plainly in his heated stare.

When he seemed satisfied, he removed his fingers from my mouth and replaced them with his tongue. His kiss was gentle yet commanding, pulling me closer and shifting me down until my back was flat against the mattress. My arms pulled deliciously tight against the restraints.

His body pressed down on mine, his defined edges and

contracting muscles sharply opposing my soft curves. Our breaths mingled, creating a shared rhythm that mirrored the beat of our hearts. When he entered me, the world around us faded into a dreamy cosmos, leaving only the intensity of the moment.

# CHAPTER 4

*Alexander*

As the gentle rays of the morning sun filtered through the curtains of *The Lucy's* luxurious master suite, I stirred and glanced at the clock on the nightstand. It was almost seven. I usually woke before sunrise, but my body clock had been thrown off these past few weeks. Going back to work would surely be an adjustment I wasn't looking forward to. I'd grown used to waking up and enjoying lazy mornings with Krystina.

I turned my head to look at the extraordinary woman lying next to me. My wife's tousled curls spilled over the pillow in a halo. The soft morning light accentuated the delicate features of her face, and a gentle smile played at the corners of her lips. She looked as if she were relishing a pleasant dream.

I watched her sleep, her chest rising and falling in a

slow, peaceful rhythm. As it happened so many mornings since our wedding, I found myself mesmerized by her beauty. The fact that she was now my partner for life filled me with a profound sense of satisfaction. My solitary days were over. She filled a void in my life that I'd unknowingly endured for far too long.

With great care, I shifted my position to avoid disturbing Krystina's slumber and went to take a shower. She'd wake soon, and I wanted breakfast ready on the main deck before we pulled up anchor. We'd sat on the polished wood deck of *The Lucy* when we first arrived at Enchanted Isle, her white sand, mysterious cliffs, and shady palms greeting us upon arrival. It seemed fitting that we also be on deck to bid her farewell.

After I showered and dressed, I stepped back into the main cabin to see Krystina sitting up in bed. She held the sheet up, barely covering her breasts, as she stared at me with wide, excited eyes.

"Are we still anchored?" she asked hurriedly.

"Yes, why?"

She let out a relieved breath with an audible *whoosh*.

"Oh, good. I was afraid we were already underway. We need to go back to the island."

"Go back? I've already given the crew instructions—"

"This will be quick. I promise," she interrupted, throwing the sheet and blankets off her. She strode naked to the closet, pulled out undergarments and a light blue sundress, and began to dress. My eyes ran up the length of her flawless legs and settled on the curvature of her impeccable ass. A vision of those limbs wrapped around me flooded my brain.

Without a second thought, I closed the distance between us in three short strides, grabbed her around the waist, and pulled her back against my chest. The thin dress she was about to slip over her head fluttered to the ground.

"Alex!"

"I need to feel you," I growled, kissing my way down her neck.

"You are insatiable!" She laughed and pushed at my shoulders. "You can have me—later. Many times, if you want. It's a long trip back to the mainland. I just need to do this one thing first."

Reluctantly, I pulled back and allowed her enough room to recover her dress. I pressed my lips together in disappointment when her gorgeous body disappeared under the cotton blend.

"I think you've forgotten the rules again, Krystina. I'm in charge, remember?"

"Yeah, yeah," she waved off, rushing to the bathroom to run a brush through her hair. After splashing some water on her face, she returned to the bedroom. "But technically, Mr. Bossy Pants, the rules ended last night since that was the last day of our honeymoon."

With my tongue in cheek, I tried to mask my amusement.

"Mr. Bossy Pants, huh?"

"I need tools," she announced without skipping a beat.

"Tools. What sort of tools?' I asked, trying to figure out where I'd failed to keep up. I was genuinely perplexed.

Her brow furrowed in concentration as she pressed a finger to her chin.

"I don't know," she eventually said with a shrug. "I'll know what I need when I see it. Is there a toolbox on board?"

"Of course. There's a large chest bolted down behind the helm."

"Perfect!"

And with that, she was off like a shot.

I followed her up to the main deck, my curiosity piqued. The sun had fully risen, casting a golden glow across the endless expanse of the open sea. I took a deep breath, inhaling the fresh ocean air as I watched my wife hustle over to a surprised-looking Isaac.

Krystina's arms waved about, and she pointed to the island. Her animated gestures reminded me of an artist painting with enthusiastic, vivid strokes. I didn't know what she was saying to the hired crew captain, but it was no matter. I was perfectly content to watch from a distance. When my wife became overly excited about something, it was usually quite entertaining to watch.

Her laughter bubbled up, a joyful symphony that resonated through the air. Then, she returned to me with a small canvas bag. I could hear metal clanking inside.

"What's in the bag?" I asked.

She winked and replied, "You'll see."

Her eyes glimmered, and her lips curled into a mischievous grin. Her excitement was infectious and almost impossible to contain. The energy around her seemed to hum with anticipation, and I couldn't help but laugh as I followed her to the dinghy that would shuttle us to shore.

When we arrived on the beach, the water gave way to

the soft, powdery sand that stretched endlessly before us. The salty breeze tousled Krystina's hair as I took her hand and helped her out of the small boat.

"Now, tell me what this is all about," I demanded, but my words carried no heat. She had my complete attention now.

"Do you remember the first day you brought me to this island?"

"Of course."

"We arrived in the morning and had a picnic breakfast of pastries and fruit—which we never finished because you decided a nearby boulder was the perfect place for a spanking. I need to find that big rock again."

I raised my eyebrows and flashed her a devilish grin.

"Itching for spanking, Mrs. Stone?"

She laughed. "No! It's just the place we christened the island, so to speak. The problem is, I can't remember where the boulder was. Do you recall the location?"

"I do. It's this way."

With her hand firmly clasped in mine, I led her down the shore toward the secluded area she was referring to.

"Look, there it is!" The energy in her voice matched the sparkle in her eyes. It was as if a well-guarded treasure chest had opened, and the contents spilled out, illuminating her entire being with an effervescent glow. Her excitement was contagious, and I couldn't help but be drawn into her world of anticipation and wonder.

I followed her gaze and saw the massive boulder standing sentinel on the beach, bathed in the shadows of the surrounding palm trees. I'd picked this location deliberately, far out of sight from any crew member on *The*

*Lucy,* knowing I'd strip Krystina bare and fuck her into oblivion.

And that was exactly what I'd done.

If I concentrated hard enough, I could still feel the stinging in my palm after I'd reddened her ass. That wasn't the only time I'd taken her on Enchanted Isle. I'd fucked my wife more times than I could count, owning her body in every way imaginable whenever an opportunity presented itself. Memories of our many beach escapades over the past few weeks rushed in. My cock jerked, and my dominant side itched to be unleashed.

"Yes, Krystina. That's the rock where we picnicked. Now, I've been patient with this unexpected excursion so far. It's time for you to tell me why you dragged us back here," I told her, this time my voice laced with authority. If she held out much longer, she would be getting that spanking whether she wanted it or not.

She closed the remaining distance to the boulder, her steps purposeful and leaving indelible marks in the sand. Seagulls glided overhead, their calls submitting to the distant crash of waves.

"I wanted to do something that would leave our mark here forever," she began. She pulled her hand from mine and reached inside her canvas bag.

When she procured chiseling tools, I raised a curious brow.

"Do I dare ask what those are for?"

She didn't answer but instead turned away from me and brought the chisel and hammer to the stone. My gaze fixated on her as she wielded the tools with precision. She moved with a captivating blend of grace and resolve, every chisel strike against the massive stone boulder radiating with purpose.

Her brow furrowed in concentration, positioning the chisel carefully until I could see her intentions. She was etching our initials into the hard surface.

I brought my attention back to her face, a slight smile forming when I saw the determination set in her jaw. Her movements were deliberate, the metallic clang of metal on metal ringing out like a passionate declaration. The stone seemed to surrender willingly to her presence as if it recognized her intent.

A profound sense of admiration and intense longing washed over me as I watched her. At that moment, I yearned to be closer to her, to somehow share in this intimate act of creation. She was a vision, a woman who commanded both admiration and desire, not only for her physical beauty but also for the depth of her character. The grace with which she etched our love made my heart constrict.

"You are incredible, angel. Do you know that?"

She paused her chiseling, frowning as she studied the carving thus far.

"Incredible isn't how I would describe this. I'm just hoping for legible," Krystina said with a laugh.

"I'm not talking about your artistic abilities, but for everything you are. You've made my life richer and more beautiful than I ever could have imagined."

She looked away from her work, her eyes meeting mine.

"You're the love of my life, Alex. This etching is more than just our initials. It's a symbol of our love, something that will endure the test of time—just like us. Now, anyone who comes here after us may see this. Evidence of our love will be etched in stone forever."

Her words carried a sense of intimacy, as if she were creating a sacred space where only a chosen few were allowed.

I pulled her into my arms, and a tender smile graced her lips. It was a smile that held a thousand unspoken words—a smile that spoke of shared memories, trials, and triumphs.

"Forever, you say?"

"Forever," she confirmed. Pressing up on her toes, she brushed her lips softly over mine. "Because forever we will be."

As the sun rose on the horizon, bringing the dawn of a new day, I felt her words in the very depths of my soul. We shared a moment of silent reflection, basking in the memories that this place held for us. Our honeymoon might be at an end, but it was merely the foundation for our journey. Forever with my new bride had only just begun.

THE END

# YULETIDE TEMPTATIONS

# THE STONE SERIES 4.5

## A SECOND CHANCE CHRISTMAS ROMANCE

*Bryan*

We had made a pact a decade ago, vowing to maintain a strictly professional relationship. But seeing Laura wrapped in a red dress made for sin ignited the suppressed flames of longing that had smoldered for years. The yearning in her gaze was undeniable.

*Laura*

After only one dance, the past came rushing back. Neither of us could resist the inevitable. All I wanted for Christmas was him. But would surrendering to our desires jeopardize everything I'd worked so arduously to attain?

# CHAPTER 1

*Laura*

The crowd applauded as I stepped away from the microphone on the stage at the Festival of Trees Gala. I ducked my head to hide my blush. Their praise was unexpected, and their reaction to my words moved me.

They were giving me too much credit. All I did was recap stories of the children helped by The Stoneworks Foundation, the non-profit organization founded by my boss, Alexander Stone. The script given to me for tonight was easy to follow. I had to walk the gala floor to ensure everything was running smoothly, shake hands with the most influential guests and donors, periodically check in on the silent auction results, and give the speech written by Krystina Stone, my boss's wife. While I typically handled things behind the scenes, I could—and was expected to—step up in a pinch.

"You killed it, Laura!" Justine Andrews, my boss's sister, said as I approached. She set her glass down on the bar next to where she stood and moved to give me a one-arm congratulatory hug. "If donors don't open their wallets after that, I'll be shocked."

I glanced over to the sixteen-foot-tall Christmas tree erected in the corner of the ballroom. The tree sparkled with thousands of white twinkle lights from the base to just above the middle section, where the pine branches began to taper in toward the top. The goal was to raise enough money throughout the night to light up the tree completely, making the crystal star topper glow to signal the fundraising goal had been met.

"All I did was read what Mrs. Stone had given me," I replied.

"Don't be so modest. I read Krystina's speech, and I know you improvised. You sounded really passionate up there."

"It's too bad she couldn't be here. I know how important this event was to her," I mused, trying to take the attention off myself.

"I know. Alex told me it was the flu, but still." Justine paused, and her lips pressed together in a tight line. "This is a major fundraiser for The Stoneworks Foundation. I assumed he would still attend tonight. I swear, the way he dotes on Krystina…"

She looked skeptical, and I stayed quiet. It wasn't my place to divulge what I knew. As the personal assistant to the billionaire real-estate investor, Alexander Stone, I was often privy to private details of his life. The story for the night was that Krystina had the flu, but I knew otherwise. My boss and his wife were experiencing fertility issues and had spent last night in a hospital after experiencing another devastating pregnancy loss. I couldn't blame them for not being here tonight.

I noticed Justine eyeing me curiously. She knew how closely I worked with her brother, so I quickly changed the subject before she could prod me for details about what might be going on.

"Sofia from the Support the Children is supposed to speak next. Hopefully, she'll get us closer to the treetop. The sooner the star lights up, the sooner I can relax."

"The speech was the hard part. At least now you can grab a drink and mingle," Justine said, holding up her peppermint martini. "You've got catching up to do! Let me grab a drink for you."

I contemplated my options and decided I wanted a classy drink to match the sophistication of my ruby-red evening gown. The rhinestone spaghetti strap dress had been a rare splurge from which my bank account would take months to recover. Alexander Stone paid me a good salary, but the Monique Lhuillier tulle dress was more than my six-figure income could responsibly support.

"I'll have what you're having," I told Justine.

"One peppermint martini coming right up!"

Angling her body toward the bar, she motioned to the bartender and then pointed at her drink. Within two minutes, he had prepared another glass rimmed with crushed peppermint candies.

"Thanks," I said to Justine as she handed me the glass.

"No problem. So, do you see that guy over there?" she asked, pointing over my shoulder. "Black suit, red tie."

I turned my head and followed the direction of her finger.

"Yeah, I see him."

"That's Matthew King from the King and Myers Law Firm. And before you ask—yes. It is *the* Matthew King, the firm's founder."

"Okay, so what about him?"

"He might be the most important person here tonight."

"Oh?"

"I'm the Head of Relations and Fundraising for The Stonework's Foundation, and he's one of the richest men in America. My job description requires that I shake the hands of people like him. But I'm hoping to snag more than his donation," she admitted with a waggle of her eyebrows. "I've been trying and failing at this dating thing long enough. Krystina pushed me back into the scene a few years after my divorce, but every time, it's been a swing and a miss. But I have a good feeling about Matthew. I've spoken to him before, and we really hit it off."

Matthew King was very attractive and would look good standing next to Justine, an effortlessly stunning woman even on her worst day. I glanced around the ballroom and thought about the rest of the guest list. Everyone here was rich. Very rich. And everyone was a potential donor with whom Justine and I needed to connect with tonight.

While I took in all the faces, I couldn't help noticing the

elegance of the crowd and the room. Chandeliers sparkled in the dim lighting. Round tables spread across the floor, with red tablecloths and centerpieces of glittering white poinsettias. As I scanned the large space, the hired band began warming up, preparing to entertain guests between the multiple speeches scheduled for the evening. A few members of Congress were in attendance. That made me happy to see. Support from the national stage was always a bonus. I made a mental note to thank them for coming at some point during the night.

My eyes continued to roam until I was suddenly overcome with the feeling of being watched. I could feel it blazing from somewhere on the other side of the room like pulsing energy. The sensation was all too familiar. I should have known better than to look, but there was nothing I could have done to stop myself. I knew who I'd discover standing there. Only one person could make me feel that sort of blistering heat.

I slowly turned, and my eyes landed on Bryan Davenport. All that invisible energy crashed like the sun's flares, searing as the flames licked my skin.

I audibly gasped, then turned away. Justine was curiously searching my face.

"Laura, what's wrong?" she asked.

The answer seemed to lodge in my throat, and I felt starved for oxygen as my gaze stayed fixed on the gorgeous man across the room. He was the one who got away—my biggest regret that I've had to face day in and day out for the better part of the past ten years. Our affair lasted only a summer, but I'd fallen hard and fast.

However, Bryan was Alexander Stone's accountant. After accepting the assistant job at Stone Enterprise, Bryan and I both agreed it was best to keep our relationship professional. It was a hard decision, but Mr. Stone wasn't the easiest man to work for back then.

It didn't matter that ten years had passed since our brief affair. Every time we were in a shared space, the sexual tension was palpable. Meetings and conferences were agonizing, with nobody but Bryan and I aware of the chemistry always bubbling just below the surface. Bryan had wanted to try and keep our relationship a secret, but I was young and career-focused, so I rejected the idea.

But oh, how I wanted him—desperately. My body ached for him.

I tore my eyes from Bryan only to see Justine staring at me expectantly.

I cleared my throat. "Oh, um…nothing is wrong. It's just that …"

I scrambled to think of an excuse.

"Just what?"

"Bryan just walked in. It reminded me that I forgot to send him an update on a recent Stone Enterprise property merger," I murmured, hoping the lie wasn't as transparent as it felt.

"That's unlike you, Laura. You don't forget things. It's why my brother values you so much."

With a light laugh, I shrugged. "Even I lose my edge sometimes."

Justine looked over my shoulder in the direction where I knew Bryan to be standing, then looked back at me.

"Your face is beat red. Is there… Oh, man. There is. Isn't there?"

"What?" I asked a little too quickly.

"Something is going on between you two."

"What makes you say that?" Even to my own ears, my tone was too heavy with feigned innocence. I never was good at lying. One look at Justine's expression, and I knew she saw through my bullshit.

She pushed away a lock of sleek black hair that had fallen free from her updo and looked at me pointedly. "You don't have to lie to me. Does Alex know?"

"There's nothing for him to know. Bryan and I had a brief fling some years back, but it was a long time ago."

"How long?"

"Ten years. Before I started working for your brother. Really, Justine. Don't make something out of nothing."

That wasn't a lie per se. It had been ten years since I'd slept with Bryan. Everything since then had simply been workplace flirtations that occasionally got out of hand. Justine didn't need to know about all the times I ran into Bryan in the office supply closet, where we just so happened to steal kisses and sometimes engage in *other* things.

Justine pressed her lips together.

"Your flushed face tells a different story, but I'd understand if you wanted to keep the relationship a secret. My brother can be a bullhead at times." She paused, and the corners of her mouth turned up in a devious smile. "He's headed this way."

"Who?"

"Bryan. Go on and have fun, Laura. My lips are

sealed." She ran her thumb and forefinger across her mouth in a fake zipper and then turned to walk away.

My gaze followed her elegant sashay as she confidently wove through the crowd toward Matthew King. It didn't matter if Justine could keep a secret. I wasn't going down that road—especially tonight. I didn't have such luxuries while I had a job to do. Networking with donors and ensuring a flawless event needed to be my focus.

I knew Bryan had already spotted me, but he was making a good show of pretending otherwise. He didn't appear to be with anyone, and I tried not to feel happy about that.

I took in his appearance as he moved about the room, only pausing to shake hands with business acquaintances. His fitted, expensive black tuxedo made him look even more broad-shouldered than usual. It was a real struggle to block out the images of what he looked like underneath all that custom-made attire. His hair was cropped short, accentuating his strong jaw and prominent cheekbones. A shiver ran down my spine.

*Damn, he looks good.*

As if he heard my thoughts, he turned and locked his eyes on mine. I felt pinned beneath them and couldn't move as he made his way toward me. His lips curved into a gorgeous, plush smile made for kissing. He studied me as if he knew what I was thinking, his expression full of something dangerous, possessive, and alive.

I suddenly found it hard to swallow. All too often, he made me wonder if this thing between us was more significant than I wanted to admit.

When he reached me, the corner of his mouth turned up in a crooked smile. "Hey, there."

I didn't know how two words could make me feel like a giddy schoolgirl, but they did. Still, I managed to keep my composure as I reached out to shake his hand in the most professional manner possible.

"It's good to see you, Mr. Davenport."

# CHAPTER 2

*Bryan*

$M$*r. Davenport.*

I stifled a smirk as I shook Laura's small hand. I liked the sound of my name on her tongue and wondered how the formality would sound on her lips in a more private, intimate setting.

I released her hand, stepped back, and discreetly gave her a once-over. Since the moment I met her, she had the power to drop me to my knees. Time hadn't altered that. Tonight, her strawberry blonde hair was styled in loose curls cascading down her back in silky waves. Even though there was a good three feet between us, I swore I could feel the warmth emitting from her very essence.

She moved with devastating grace, her body wrapped in a red satin dress meant for sin. She was so stunning that I couldn't think straight, a reaction I seemed to have whenever she was around. It was an intense lust so forceful that it made me dizzy.

"You look amazing. Beautiful, as always," I told her quietly so as not to be overheard by any bystander.

"Thank you. Right back atcha'," she replied with a playful smile. "You're a little late to the party. They started passing hors d'oeuvres over an hour ago. If you catch a waiter, I'm sure they'll have fresh stuff in the kitchen."

"I'm fine, but thanks. I already ate. I honestly wasn't even planning on coming tonight. It was a last-minute decision."

She cocked her head to the side, her blue eyes sparkling with curiosity. "Oh? What made you change your mind?"

"I heard Alex was MIA tonight, so I took advantage of the opportunity to come see you," I answered matter-of-factly.

"Bryan…" She trailed off. Her warning tone was clear, but I refused to heed it. The opportunity to see her outside of the office was rare. The no fraternization policy at Stone Enterprise made sure of that. Tonight was a rarity, and I just wanted to have a bit of fun.

Glancing up at the stage, I noticed the band had finished their warmup and was about to strike up their first song. Taking the glass Laura was holding, I placed it on the bar.

"Please. One dance, my lady," I said with an exaggerated bow and a teasing wink.

Her irritated expression melted away to a smile. Then she laughed softly, and the sound reminded me of a different time—when she'd been mine, even if it wasn't meant to be.

However, instead of taking my hand, she stepped back.

"I'm sorry, Bryan. I can't. While the band is playing, I need to be on the floor talking to donors. They'll play for thirty minutes, and then we'll break for our next speaker. Do you see that Christmas tree over there?" she asked, pointing to the large artificial pine in the corner. "I need to make the star light up. I can't do that if I spend all night dancing with you."

"Just one dance," I insisted, wrapping my arm around her waist and leading her to the dance floor.

"Bryan..." she said in a cautionary tone.

I chuckled and pulled her against me just as the band's female vocalist began to sing a cover of Dean Martin's "I've Got My Love to Keep Me Warm." Splaying my palm firmly against her lower back, I guided her into a dance.

"You're stunning."

She blushed but tried to conceal it with a roll of her eyes.

"Stop that," she scolded.

"Just take the compliment, Laura. You're the most beautiful woman in the room."

I felt a shiver run down her body, and I grinned in satisfaction. After ten years of flirting, I knew when I was getting to her. I thought it was time we ended this cat-and-mouse game we'd been playing for far too long. I was tired of the forbidden touches when nobody was looking. Things at Stone Enterprise had changed ever since Alexander and Krystina got married. Alexander was more than my boss—he was my friend, and I'd had a front-row seat to his transformation. Krystina softened his hard edges, and I truly believed he'd be okay with Laura and I trying to make a go of things.

The problem was Laura. Forever the professional, breaking down those walls she tried so hard to hold up would be difficult. I'd spent the better part of the past six months trying to convince her we should try again and go public about our feelings. But she'd refused to listen or entertain any such notion so far.

Her body moved with mine to the music as I led her around the dance floor. Our feet shuffled in time effortlessly as if she were made to be dancing in my arms.

"Laura," I murmured, leaning in so my voice was barely a whisper against her ear. "I want to—"

"No, Bryan," she interjected. "I know you well enough to know what you are about to say. Please don't. This isn't the time nor the place for serious discussions."

"So when is the right time? It's loud in here. Nobody can hear us."

She pressed her lips together tightly as a civil war waged in her eyes.

"I don't want to overcomplicate things—and I don't just mean tonight. I know what you want, but our jobs could be impacted if things go south. It could mess up everything I've worked so hard for."

"And if they go right?"

She let the question linger as if she were collecting her thoughts.

"What about your other women?"

"What women? I'm not seeing anyone."

"Maybe not now, but I've seen the emails between you,

Alexander, and the rest of your pack. Rarely did any of you boys spend a night alone."

I studied her expression as we moved ever so slowly across the dance floor, and suddenly, the reasons she continued to deny a relationship all made sense.

"You think I'm a playboy," I stated flatly.

"Are you going to say you're not?"

I sighed, unsure if there was a way to justify how I'd lived my life for too many years. Me and my friends, Alex, Matteo, and Stephen, were anything but angels. Laura was right. There had been women—a lot of them. But things had shifted over the past few years. Alexander got married. Matteo didn't seem interested in shenanigans anymore. Stephen was overworked and didn't go out as often as he used to.

And then there was me.

Every woman I'd been with after Laura were bodies I'd used to pass the time while waiting for her. As horrible as that sounded, it was the truth as I knew it. I just wasn't sure if she'd accept it.

"The other women never mattered, Laura. None of them fit right because they weren't you. I wanted you the whole time. Always. It was just you."

Her expression went from astonishment to hopeful to sadness in a split second.

Before I could say more, the band slowed it down with a rendition of "Wintersong" by Sarah McLachlan. If I wasn't mistaken, I thought I saw a glimmer of tears in Laura's eyes.

*Fuck.*

The last thing I wanted to do was make her cry.

"That was one dance, Bryan. Thank you, but I have to go now," Laura whispered and pulled away.

"Wait," I said, reaching out to her.

She didn't pull away again but let me guide her slowly back into my arms.

"Just one more," she whispered the warning like she didn't really mean it.

I could barely breathe as the female vocalist sang. The song lyrics were sad and longing, fitting for the moment. I began to question why I didn't push a relationship with Laura sooner. Denying how we felt simply because of workplace restrictions was ridiculous.

I could feel her heart thudding in her chest. It matched the beat of mine. She knew what I was feeling—she felt it, too. A lump formed in my throat, and I swallowed, wanting to beat myself for wasting so much damn time.

"Laura, I know it might be hard to believe, but none of the other women matter. When we agreed to go our separate ways, I had no clear direction other than my career. You need to know that—"

She silenced me by placing a finger on my lips.

"Shhh…I believe you, Bryan. Let's just enjoy the dance."

We fell quiet and moved to the music, her body moving with ease against mine. The song ended too soon, and I didn't want to let her go. When she began to pull away a second time, I didn't hold her back. She had a job to do tonight. I was familiar with these events and the importance of them. It would be wrong of me to monopolize more of her time.

"Duty calls."

"Yes, it does," she agreed. "I need that star to light up before the night's end."

"What happens once it does?"

"Then my time becomes my own again, and I can relax," she said with a light laugh.

"Time for another dance, maybe?"

She stared at me for a beat, her expression impenetrable. Then, without answering, she turned and walked away.

I must have stood there like a fool for another three minutes at least, stunned by the connection I had to this woman. I shouldn't have been surprised. It had always been there, but now it was burning brighter than the sun. I shook my head, forced myself to leave the dance floor, and headed to the bar.

"I need a fucking drink," I muttered under my breath.

After ordering a Henry McKenna Single Barrel neat, I scanned the crowd until I spotted Laura again. I watched her work the group for a while, completely in awe of her ability to move efficiently around the expansive ballroom, never lingering too long with one guest before moving on to the next.

She was beautiful—the whole package—and not just in appearance. It was her entire persona and the way she presented herself. She had so much goodness, and I wondered if she even knew it.

The music stopped, and another speaker took the stage, but I barely heard a word of the speech. I was too focused on Laura. I never wanted her more than I did right then—to feel her pressed against me in another dance. I recalled the feeling of her tight body, the way she moved with me in time to the music, and I began to envision more. Being with her again. Inside her. Hearing her scream my name. I could almost picture her just as she was ten years ago, eyes wide with desire. I wanted to see that look on her face now.

I glanced over at the Christmas tree. It was more than three-quarters of the way lit. The sooner that tree topper glowed, the sooner I could have Laura all to myself.

On impulse, I headed to the area where workers were accepting donations.

"How much more do you need to make that thing light up?" I asked the teenage girl working behind the table.

She looked down at the computer screen before her, then back up at me.

"We hope to raise two hundred fifty thousand tonight and have about nineteen more to go. We're well ahead of the projected schedule!" she announced cheerfully.

"Oh, nineteen hundred dollars isn't too bad."

"Oh no, sir. Nineteen *thousand* more to go. Not nineteen hundred."

*Nineteen thousand.*

I nearly cringed. That amount would take a sizable chunk from the deposit I planned to make on a late model Sea Ray boat I'd been eyeing up at Montauk Marina.

"Would you like to donate, sir?" the girl prompted, eyeing the line of people standing behind me. "You can do it right here, or we have a website where you can donate anonymously through your smartphone."

*Fuck it.*

Laura was more important than a boat. Without further hesitation, I pulled out my wallet.

"Does the website take credit cards?"

# CHAPTER 3

*Laura*

The entire ballroom erupted into cheers, causing me to pause the conversation I was having with Kimberly Melbourne, an interior designer who'd just been commissioned to remodel The Stoneworks Foundation headquarters. I turned around to see what the commotion was all about and saw the star at the top of the tree had lit. Bright rays of light shot in every direction, illuminating the entire room.

"Well done, Laura," Kimberly said.

I looked back at her, my mouth curving in an ear-splitting grin.

"Thank you!"

"It's early in the night, too. Mr. Stone will be pleased. I guess you don't need a donation from me after all."

"Oh, no. You're not off the hook," I teased. "We can always use more."

"I know, I know," she said with a chuckle. "I'll head over to the donation table right now."

When she walked away, I scanned the room for Justine. She was standing at a high-top table with Matthew King. They clinked glasses in apparent celebration over having reached the goal of the evening. I smiled to myself. Today was a good day.

The band took the stage for another set, starting with an upbeat tune to match the crowd's excitement.

"Now that your work is complete, I believe you have more time for dancing," said a low voice behind me.

I slowly turned to see Bryan behind me. I smiled, overcome with excitement from the jubilation emitting throughout the room. Not waiting for me to respond, he grabbed me by the arm and twirled me onto the floor with the other dancers.

Another hour passed in what only seemed like five minutes. We danced and talked, our conversation jumping from one topic to the next. Some dances were fast, while others were slow, but the slow dances differed from the ones we shared earlier. A buzz in the air made it seem like everything had a sexual undertone. The tension from earlier was gone. Bryan's flirtations were deliberate, as were his hands, which shamelessly roamed over my back and hips. He made all the little hairs on my body stand on end, and my nipples went painfully hard every time I pressed against him. My body seemed to hum to life with only a single look from him.

After a while, we both needed a break and headed to the bar. Once our drinks came, Bryan turned to me and leaned close to my ear.

"Room twelve-ten. Fifteen minutes," he whispered. Then he pressed a plastic card to my palm before leaving me alone and slack-jawed with a keycard to a hotel room in my hand.

As I stared down at the black plastic, my heart thudded loudly in my ears. I wasn't naïve. I knew what the invitation meant without him even saying it.

*I can't leave and go to his room. Or can I?*

I was flirting with danger. This could have a negative impact on my job. Overwhelming panic consumed me, and I wasn't sure if I was ready to give in to him. But the more immediate concern was the gala. I didn't know if it was responsible to leave just yet.

I searched the room for Justine, but she was nowhere to be found.

*Dammit!*

I took a long swig of peppermint martini number two. I wasn't a big drinker, so having already consumed a martini and a couple of glasses of champagne, this one went straight to my head. I set the glass on the bar, knowing I needed a clear head.

I looked around the room again. Everything seemed to be going well, if not winding down for the night. Many guests still mingled, but several were heading to the coat room.

After ten minutes of indecision, I knew what I had to do.

MY HANDS TREMBLED as I fumbled to insert the keycard into the slot of the hotel room door. When I entered, I found more than just the average hotel room. Bryan had reserved a suite with a sitting area and a separate bedroom. Music played softly in the background.

Bryan stood near the couch, and the entire space seemed consumed by his presence. He'd removed his tuxedo jacket, leaving it tossed haphazardly on the back of a settee. His tie was loosened at the neck, and one hand rested in his pants pocket while the other ran anxiously over the top of his head. His presence pummeled me, so powerful and raw, and energy seemed to crawl up the walls.

His eyes showed hesitations as he took me in, but there was also desire.

"I'm glad you came," he said huskily.

Memories of the past ten years ricocheted through the depths of my being, causing a shiver to race down my spine.

"I'm glad, too," I breathed.

"Strawberry?" he asked, pointing toward the coffee table.

My gaze followed his finger toward a platter of strawberries, each artfully arranged to surround a bowl of whipped cream. Champagne had been poured, the little bubbles slowly rising to the surface of two crystal glasses.

I hadn't expected this. It was seduction in every sense of the word. I had a feeling he'd been planning this, or something like it, for a while.

"I, um…" I faltered, words just seeming to ramble from my mouth. "Sure."

I felt rooted to the spot, undecided on my next move. But, as it turned out, I didn't have to decide because Bryan did it for me. He was already moving closer, possession in each measured stride. He leaned in and pressed the gentlest kiss to the curve of my neck. His spicy and masculine scent clouded my senses. I trembled when he reached up, his fingers softly brushing along the side of my cheek. I dared to look into his eyes only to see them swirling with something fierce.

"Let's sit down."

He led me over to the couch, and we sat. I stared at the plate of strawberries, my mind in a daze. I blinked once, then twice, trying unsuccessfully to break free from the spell he seemed to have me under.

"Bryan," I began, attempting to find balance. But the strawberry he brought to my lips silenced anything I might have said.

"Taste," he demanded.

*Oh, God…*

So much more was laced in that one little command. My already pounding heart began to race faster and faster. Every dirty fantasy I'd ever had about Bryan over the years wanted to come to life right here in this room. I thought I might combust just from the images conjuring in my head.

"Bryan, I know you said Mr. Stone, er…Alexander might not care, but—"

"Don't. We are two consenting adults who don't need permission from a rule fanatic," he interrupted. Then he sighed. "Look, I love my friend, but he can be a bit over the top. What you and I have together has been going on for too long. We owe it to ourselves to give in to our feelings and see where it takes us."

Stark vulnerability oozed from his truth. My throat tightened with an onslaught of emotions, making my mouth dry. I unconsciously ran my tongue over my lips to moisten them so I could speak. Bryan's eyes dropped and followed the path of my tongue before finally making their way back up to mine. As I was about to respond, his lips crashed down on mine.

I didn't even attempt to protest, surrendering to his hot, merciless kiss. Our tongues quickly found each other, his more aggressive than mine. He had the ferocity of a hot-blooded male taking complete and utter control.

"Surrender yourself to me, Laura. Please," he murmured feverishly against my lips. "Can you do that?"

Layer by layer, he was stripping me bare, peeling away the hurt to expose a part of me that I'd kept buried for far too long.

"Yes," I whispered between kisses.

His hard contours pressed against the softness of my body, and I found myself reaching up to thread my hands through his cropped hair. He groaned when I tugged on the short ends, pulling me tighter against him. I'm not sure when or how it happened so quickly, but we went from kissing to fervently groping each other in a matter of minutes.

My fingers found the buttons of his shirt, and I worked my way down, the desperate need to feel his bare flesh under my palms becoming all-consuming. He caressed a hand down my back, along the zipper of my dress, and settled at my waist. Shivers raced down my spine, wishing he'd tug the zipper down. He made me want things that I'd never wanted with anyone else. Every time he was near, I felt an unexplainable connection between us, like an invisible line that remained unchanged over time.

Bryan pulled back slightly, leaving us both panting. He was a disheveled mess, his hair sticking up wildly. His shirt was twisted, only having been partially removed. His chiseled abdomen rippled as he shrugged impatiently out of the rest. Once it was off, he reached for me again.

Pure, uninhibited lust raced through my veins like a potent drug. He was all around me, his presence thick and consuming in a way only he could be. It had been so long since I'd wanted—and I mean, really wanted—anyone. I'd fantasized so many times about what it would be like to be with Bryan again. Our stolen kisses had never been enough throughout the years, but I never thought I'd allow this to happen again.

I closed my eyes as he pressed soft kisses down my neck. He exuded testosterone, drugging my senses until I was high on him. I soared, my blood heating, my flesh on fire.

When he brought his lips to mine, he hovered over them, barely touching. My lips parted, and we breathed together, slowly inhaling each other's need. It was as potent as ever. Only he could make me feel this alive. I gave in and felt my body melt into him, burying all fears and letting go of every ounce of resistance.

# CHAPTER 4

*Bryan*

I sensed the moment she surrendered. Her cheeks flushed, and her eyes darkened, the color turning a deep blue and brimming with possibilities. I knew I should take my time despite the electric heat burning through my system. I had planned to take her to dinner first, then maybe to see a show on Broadway. I had wanted to give her romance like I never had the chance to over the years.

But then tonight happened. After feeling her warm body pressed against mine and her hips gyrating against me on the dance floor, I threw the thought of taking things slow right out the window.

Now, I could barely believe she was here in my arms. What Laura and I had was nothing but pure and good. It was real. I'd missed her, and I had missed this.

"I waited too long. Just too damn long," I whispered against her mouth before running my tongue over her perfect lips, demanding she open to me. I kissed her. Tenderly. Passionately. Desperately. I wanted her to feel everything I felt—to feel the relief from finally having something we'd denied ourselves.

My arms banded tightly around her, and I hauled her to my chest, carrying her tight body to the bedroom. I never took my lips from hers, guiding her as I plundered her mouth. Once there, I carefully set her back on her feet, turning her around to press her back against my chest. I held her close, palm splayed across her firm abdomen as I leaned in to graze her ear. My breath was hot on her neck as she tilted her head so I could nibble the curve of her shoulder. A shiver rocked her body, and she moaned.

"Bryan..." she sighed and tried to turn to face me. I stopped her, keeping her back firmly against me. I wasn't in a hurry. I wanted to savor every moment with her.

"I don't want to be rushed. I want to take my time and make you feel good."

"I need to touch you," she persisted.

"We'll get there. But first, I want to feel every curve, to memorize you with my hands. With my tongue. I want to taste every inch of you."

She shuttered again as I moved my hand up her back to the zipper of her dress. Slowly, I tugged the red material down to expose the delicate curve of her spine. Then, looping a finger under each strap at her shoulder, I slid them down until the silk pooled at her feet.

I pressed my lips to her shoulder, trailing soft kisses along the hollow at the side of her throat as I reached around to cup her breasts through the black strapless bra.

The lacy material was rough against my palms, yet it was still sexy. Intimate. And all woman.

I groaned my approval as my cock strained in my pants. I thought I might come on the spot. I restrained the mad desire I felt for her, forcing myself to do exactly as I'd promised, and went through the motions of memorizing every delicious inch of her body. My mouth moved across her shoulders, working my way down her back and over her hips.

More lace. And a thong, no less.

"You're unbelievable. You don't know what you do to me," I uttered as I cupped her ass and raked my tongue over the curve of one cheek, then the other, before moving down and up each of her legs. "Your taste. Your scent."

Working back up her body, I finally turned her to face me. Pure lust thrummed through my veins, and I felt my jaw tighten, desperate to see everything underneath the few scraps of black, sexy lace. I reached around to her back with slow, purposeful grace and unclasped her bra. Perfect mounds and pink nipples spilled free.

"Oh, God," she gasped.

I cupped her neck and ran my tongue down the base of her throat, over her clavicle, until I captured one hardened peak in my teeth. I relished her startled cry as I rolled the other nipple between my thumb and finger. I lured her back toward the bed until the backs of her knees hit the mattress. Legs buckling beneath her, she sat down.

"Lie back. I'm going to take care of you," I told her.

She hesitated, her eyes fraught with an emotion I couldn't identify, and my stomach sank. I nearly swore, hoping like hell she wasn't having second thoughts now.

"Laura, don't look at me like that. Don't tell me to stop."

"I won't. I'm just… I want this, Bryan. I need it—I need you. No more talking. Just touch me, please."

"No talking? I'm sure I can think of something to keep my mouth occupied," I teased as I coaxed her back, eager to remove that final barrier of clothing so I could taste her.

Sliding down the lace thong, inch by beautiful inch, I tossed it aside and dropped to my knees between her legs. Grabbing her ankles, I pushed her legs apart, carefully assessing her expression as I did. Desire pooled deep in her ocean-blue eyes, the delicate blush moving from her cheeks to her breasts.

Tearing my gaze from her face, I allowed myself finally to look down at her now exposed sex.

So fucking gorgeous.

I slid the pad of one finger gently over her clit. Her back immediately arched, and a gasp wrenched from her throat.

"Oh!"

I parted her folds and slowly sank one finger inside her heated well, a sharp hiss escaping me.

"God, you're exquisite. So wet. So ready. So damned tight." I slid another finger in, stroking her inner walls while my thumb traced slow, leisurely circles over that pulsing bundle of nerves.

She gasped again, and I sank low, unable to go another minute without tasting her.

"Tell me you want me, baby. Tell me you want this."

"Yes, yes! I want it," she unashamedly begged.

Wedging my shoulders between her legs, I rested my

face against her inner thigh and inhaled her sweet scent. Dipping down, I swiped my tongue over her entrance in one long lick. She tasted as good as she smelled.

Her hands reached down and grasped the ends of my hair, searching for something to hang onto as I explored every nook and crevice of her most intimate parts. I dipped into her core before lapping her oh-so-sweet spot, making her writhe beneath me. I pressed my tongue flat against her, rolling until that beautiful nub began to pulse. It was only a matter of time before she came apart.

"That's it. Let go, baby. Let me taste you on my tongue. I want you to feel it. I want you to feel everything I was meant to make you feel."

"Oh, God. Please!"

She pushed up against my mouth. I glanced up to find her head lolling from side to side, strawberry blonde hair splayed out on the bed, desperate for the release that was so near. Laura, without inhibition, was intoxicating. I could drown in her. Her hips bucked, but I held her still, bringing her to new heights.

Her body stiffened, and she inhaled sharply. When she came, she screamed my name, and it was the most glorious thing I'd ever heard.

I toed off my shoes and shed my pants, leaving only my boxer briefs in place. I eased her body up the bed and blanketed her with my weight, sinking us deeper into the mattress. My throbbing cock pressed against her abdomen as I worked my hand up her thigh, peppering light kisses along her collarbone.

"Do you feel how hard you make me?" I whispered.

She looked into my eyes, and I saw something shift.

"I feel you, Bryan. I want you more than anything. I'm accepting the risk—not just with my job, but with my heart. Be careful with it."

*Christ, this woman will be my undoing.*

There was something about the way she curved into me, the way she smelled like jasmine and sunshine, that made everything else in life fall away. She was the only woman I could ever remember wanting to hold on to for more than a fleeting moment, and I knew, without a shadow of a doubt, that I'd be careful with her.

"We belonged together. I'm not about to fuck it up—not now after you finally agreed to give us a chance. I'll stop now if you want to slow things down, but you have to know that I've never wanted anything more than I want you right now."

She reached up to cup my face.

"Then what are you waiting for?" she asked.

Not wanting to spend another moment hesitating, I got up from the bed and opened the nightstand drawer to remove the box of condoms I had placed there earlier.

"Were you planning this all along, Mr. Davenport?" she teased, but there was also a hint of suspicion in her question.

I chuckled.

"I know how it looks, but no. I shot over to the corner store while you were schmoozing donors. After dancing with you, I figured I should grab them just in case."

I shed my boxers and made quick work of the condom. Before climbing back onto the bed, I took a moment to appreciate her nude body spread out before me. Laura was like a feast I couldn't wait to devour. She was always beautiful, but a naked, luminous Laura was something poets could write sonnets about.

I crawled up her body, and she bent her legs, cradling me. Positioning myself at her entrance, I pushed forward, barely sliding through the arousal between her lips. Her slender arms clung to my neck encouragingly, and I drove all the way in.

I sucked in a gasp so hard it made my lungs hurt. The effect she had on me hit me like an earthquake. Lacing my fingers through her hair, I captured her mouth with mine.

"Oh, God. Bryan," she whimpered as my forehead rocked against hers.

I continued to push into her, our words hushed as our bodies moved together.

"Nobody has ever fit me the way you do. Night after night, for ten long years, you crept into my dreams. I dreamed about touching you. Kissing you. Fucking you. I let go of you once for a stupid reason. I won't do it again," I declared, the words a breath of a whisper against her lips.

She moved her hips, matching my thrusts as she gripped my shoulders. It was as if she couldn't get close enough, and it was a feeling I understood all too well. I had to remind myself to go slow when every fiber of my being wanted to fuck her hard and claim her as mine once and for all.

Her nails raked down my back to my ass. I felt their bite against my skin as she made those little gasping noises that made me impossibly hard. Nothing had ever felt or sounded so damn good. She was perfect. There was just the right amount of give-and-take as I drove into her deep and hard. The air in the room seemed to come alive—the energy and the connection were the most genuine thing I'd ever felt. I could worship her all night long.

I tried to keep some modicum of control, but it was useless. I could feel her desire building as she moaned my name. Our bodies were slick with sweat, pleasure-bound, and full of need. When I felt her start to fall apart again, I pinned her arms above her head. I plunged into her, possessing her, the tightening of her perfect body making me feel like I could live forever.

My body raced, my dick pulsing with need, hard and desperate. Hunger ravaged my veins, and every muscle in my body tightened, rippling with an unbearable force. I slammed home, and my world flashed white. So bright. A blinding light that left me quaking in her arms.

We lay there panting for what seemed like hours, but it was probably only minutes. After a time, I rolled off her, and she snuggled into the crook of my arm. Her arm draped across my torso, so warm and familiar. It was where she was meant to be.

She looked up at me, her eyes searching for something. What it was, I didn't know. I reached out and brushed my thumb across the bottom of her swollen lip. Old hopes mingled with new ones filled my mind. They were thoughts of what could be.

When she reached out and pinched my arm, I jolted. It wasn't a hard pinch, but it surprised me nonetheless.

"What was that for?"

"I've dreamed about this, but I didn't think either of us would allow it to happen again. But now... I don't know what to think. Tonight feels like a fairy tale—as if Christmas magic brought my dreams to life, and when I wake up, it will all be over. The pinch is just to make sure you're really here."

"Baby, this is as real as it gets."

I leaned in and pressed a slow kiss to her lips, hoping to convey everything I was thinking with this one simple act.

In a way, tonight was the conclusion to our unique version of the Christmas Carol. The message in the Charles Dickens tale is that even someone as lost as Ebenezer Scrooge could be saved if he seized the gift of a second chance. Laura and I had chosen our career ambitions over happiness, but we didn't have to continue on that path.

I truly believed holiday magic was gifting us a second chance. I didn't have the Ghost of Christmas Past, Present, or Future to guide me, but in my heart, I knew my future with Laura was bright with possibility. All we needed to do was grab hold and enjoy the ride.

# MEETING STONE

## ALTERNATE POINT OF VIEW CHAPTER

*Meeting Stone* is an alternate point of view of Alexander meeting Krystina for the first time in *Heart of Stone.*

# CHAPTER 1

*Alexander*

I crossed the entrance of Wally's grocery store with a sense of purpose. Walter Roberts, the store owner, trailed closely behind me. With him was some irritating employee that I was hoping to ditch sometime soon. His name was Jim something or another, a nuisance who prattled on as if he held a position of importance.

Ignoring him, I took in my surroundings, noting that the establishment needed modernization and renovations if it were to survive.

"As you can see, we've made significant improvements to check outlines," Walter pointed out. "However, our registers could use an update to accommodate current technology."

"Hmmm," I mused, more to myself than him.

The establishment required more than just a computer

system overhaul. I was uncertain about my commitment to investing in this failing grocer, but the impact it would have on the community was undeniable. The only question was how much I was willing to put on the line.

I was about to ask Walter about the store's security system but was interrupted when I heard a loud thud and the sound of a woman yelping from somewhere nearby.

"Damn planogram!" she cursed.

I directed my gaze toward the source of the disturbance, and a captivating figure caught my eye. A stunning brunette with legs that seemed to go on forever stood with both hands firmly planted on her head. She was tall and curvy in all the right places. She wasn't my usual type, but something was appealing about her. Her accusatory gaze was fixed on a poorly designed supermarket display, and a frown was etched on her forehead.

A hint of a smirk played at the corners of my lips as she directed her attention to her damp shirt and the cell phone lying haphazardly on the floor in what appeared to be a pool of coffee with milk. When she reached down to retrieve it, another expletive escaped her lips.

"Son of a bitch!"

I frowned with displeasure.

*Quite the foul mouth on that one.*

Her eyes scanned the area and came to rest on me, Walter Roberts, and the minion he had in tow. A flush of embarrassment could be seen creeping up her neck and illuminating her cheeks as it became apparent that her outburst had not gone unnoticed. When her eyes locked on mine, her delectable blush deepened.

"Oh, my! Are you okay?" Walter Roberts asked, interrupting my vision of peeling every stitch of clothing from her body. I glanced over at him. Alarmed over what had happened, Walter ran his hands over his thinning gray hair.

I looked back at the woman, moving toward her at the precise moment she decided to take a step back. What happened next seemed to have transpired in slow motion. One minute she was upright, and the next, she fell unceremoniously to the ground. She had slipped on the spilled coffee and was going down hard. I could have done nothing to stop her fall if I had tried.

Hurrying toward her, I bent to place a hand on her shoulder. Her head tilted to meet my gaze, and she stared for what seemed like a long while. I took the opportunity to access her quickly.

I'd always defined a beautiful woman to be someone with breathtaking physical features who moved with effortless grace and commanded attention from everyone in the room. I appreciated beauty that came from a unique combination of facial symmetry, luminous skin, captivating eyes, and full lips.

This woman appeared to have all of that and more—except grace. Graceful, she was not.

As she stared back, the innocence of her spirit touched something within me, and I felt a slight shiver run down my spine. The look we shared was intense, and unlike anything I'd ever experienced. I found myself uncharacteristically mesmerized.

*Who is this woman, and why did she unnerve me so?*

Roberts spoke again, breaking my strange connection to this mystery woman.

"Did you hear me? I asked if you were okay. This is Mr. Stone," he told her. "He's trying to help you up."

"Mr. Stone?" she asked, seeming dazed yet never tearing her eyes from mine. Whatever I was feeling, there was no doubt the feeling was mutual.

"That's correct. And you might be?" I asked, lowering myself to a kneeling position beside her. My fingers glided down the length of her arm, lingering at the bend of her elbow. I locked eyes with her once more, and the way her pulse fluttered at my nearness was impossible to overlook.

She didn't answer, so I repeated the question.

"And your name is?"

A million little things seemed to flash in her eyes, and I couldn't help wondering what she was thinking. I always loved the challenge of figuring out one's mind, especially a woman's. One female was so vastly different from the next. They were complex individuals with unique thought processes, making some more predictable than others. Deciphering facial expressions was the key to understanding the messaging behind any woman's words. Actively listening to voice tones combined with body language also left subtle cues that could reveal what a woman was thinking. The problem was that the woman before me was motionless and seemed rendered speechless. As hard as I tried, I couldn't get a read on her. Her racing pulse was the only insight I had. At the very least, it could signal that I affected her.

"I'm K-Krys," she eventually stammered. Then she

licked her lips and began twisting her hands. My gaze narrowed, her nervous fidgeting making my cock twitch.

"Krys? Is that short for something else?" I asked, needing a distraction from that damn fidgeting while also being bothered by the shortened version of her name.

"It's short for Krystina. Krystina Cole," said Walter's minion.

Irritated, I slowly turned my head toward him and pressed my lips together in a tight line as his name finally came to me.

*Jim. Jim McNamara.*

He was an annoying little big that I just wanted to squash.

"Why, thank you, Mr. McNamara, for speaking on Miss Cole's behalf. However, I would have preferred to hear it from Miss Cole herself," I replied tersely.

"Well, Miss Cole appears to have lost her voice," McNamara retorted, his voice laden with sarcasm.

"Jim!" Walter snapped.

I ignored the antics of both men and turned back to Krystina Cole. Standing, I held out my hand for her to take.

"Please, allow me to help you up," I offered.

She looked up at me, eyes as wide as a deer in headlights, before offering me her trembling hand. Our eyes locked, and I watched her blush deepen. My eyes narrowed. All I could think about was taking her over my knee and making her perfect little ass match the flush in her cheeks.

*Fuck, Stone. Get a grip. You don't even know this woman.*

Clasping her hand tightly, I pulled her to her feet and

wrapped my arm around her waist to steady her. Her body pressed firmly against mine, and I heard her audible intake of breath. We were so close that I could smell the shampoo she'd used that morning. It was soft, like vanilla mixed with sunshine.

"I'm sure she could have gotten up on her own, you know," Jim said irritably, reminding me that I wasn't alone with this enigma of a woman. Spanking her would have to wait. We had an audience—in a very, very public place.

I removed my arm from around Miss Cole's waist, took a step back, and released her hand. I turned toward Jim, not bothering to hide my menacing glare. I half wondered if he had a thing for his female colleague. If he did, I couldn't blame him. Beautiful was too mundane of a word to describe Kristina Cole. She was nothing short of stunning, and the idea of him laying a single finger on her sparked irrational jealousy. It grew stronger from somewhere deep in my being, and I felt my gaze darken. The annoying grocery store employee cowered and took a few steps back.

Having noticed the tension on the verge of boiling over, Walter Roberts made a loud show of clearing his throat and quickly dismissed Jim to do another task in a different department.

"But, Mr. Roberts, I was supposed to—" Jim started in protest.

"Jim, please go help Melanie. Now. She's alone in the department today, and I'm sure she could use a hand unloading the truck that just arrived," Roberts ordered Jim. His tone was stern, and I appreciated the authority he displayed. Walter Roberts wasn't a pushover. That fact put my mind at ease, solidifying my decision to invest in the struggling grocer.

McNamara stomped away, and I suppressed a small smile.

*Good riddance.*

Turning my attention back to Krystina, the smile I'd held back broke through ever so slightly as I took in her appearance. Before that moment, I hadn't had a chance to appreciate how amusing the entire situation really was. She was clearly humiliated standing there in an espresso-stained Wally's t-shirt. It was plastered to her torso, accentuating every curve and line of her small waist. I found her embarrassment endearing.

Much to my disappointment, she began slowly backing away. Walter Roberts started rambling about terrible planograms and schematics that needed changing, but I barely listened to his words. At that moment, my sole focus was on Krystina Cole.

When her eyes locked with mine, I felt the corners of my mouth turn up. Then, holding up a finger to silence Walter, I gave a short nod of farewell to Krystina.

"Have a good day, Miss Cole. I'll be seeing you soon," I promised.

I watched her walk away. Actually, run away would have been a more accurate description. I smiled to myself, intrigued by the very embarrassed yet delectable Miss Cole. Her pouty mouth, round chocolate-colored eyes, and ready blush made my dick twitch.

"I'm so sorry about that, Mr. Stone. Krystina and I were just discussing how the display needed changing," Walter continued with a nervous laugh as if he somehow believed I was paying attention to him. "It just goes to show how much our vendors know about merchandising."

"Yes, indeed," I murmured absently, my eyes still following the captivating woman as she continued her way to the front doors of the supermarket chain. "Walter, tell me about that woman. I assume she's an employee?"

"Oh, yes. Krystina has worked here for years. Great eye for merchandising, that one does," Walter Roberts observed, following my gaze. "I hate the thought of losing her."

"Is she going somewhere?"

"Hopefully not, but I'm sure it won't be long before she lands herself a fancy marketing job," Roberts said regretfully.

"Marketing, you say?" I asked, turning my attention back to the store owner. He had my attention now.

"Yes, I believe that was her major," he answered cautiously, then narrowed his eyes at me suspiciously.

*Hmm… protective of her, are we?*

I glanced back again, only to barely glimpse her tight, jean-clad ass, as the front doors closed behind her. I wished I had more time to converse with her, but between her fall and the annoying store clerk, there had been little opportunity for talking before she took off.

*That clerk… what was his name again? Jim something or another?*

I didn't know why I repeatedly couldn't recall his name. Perhaps it was because I knew he was irrelevant. Still, the possibility of him being her boyfriend bothered me more than it should. I really hoped he wasn't.

Walter Roberts cleared his throat annoyingly as if he

were trying to remind me of the business at hand. It was no matter. I knew a wise investment when I saw it. There was no need to dawdle in the store any longer. After all, time was money. And while I had plenty of the latter, I was now pressed for time. If I stayed much longer, I wouldn't be able to catch up with Krystina Cole.

"I'll have my lawyers draw up a proposal, one I think you will find satisfactory. We can discuss things further at a later date," I shrugged off.

"Well, er...," Roberts faltered. "Mr. Stone, don't you want to see the rest of the store? Or perhaps some of our other locations?"

"No, I believe I've seen enough here to decide. I'll be in touch," I dismissed.

I left Walter Roberts gaping after me as I made my way to the front entrance. Then, pulling my cell out of my jacket pocket, I hit the number one on speed dial.

"Hale, did you see which way the brunette went?" I asked into the phone.

"Which brunette, sir? There must have been a hundred that walked by in the past thirty minutes," my security detail told me.

I pushed through the turnstile front doors of the grocery store and glanced back and forth down the street. There was no sign of her.

*Damn it!*

"Ah, forget it, Hale. I'm finished here. Bring the car around."

*I'll catch up with you eventually, Miss Cole.*

# MUSIC IN BOOKS

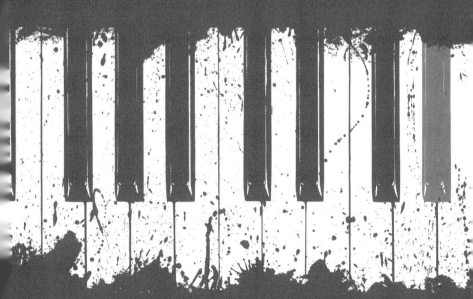

# THE STONE SERIES PLAYLISTS

# HEART OF STONE PLAYLIST

## Listen to it on Spotify!

"Wait Up (Boots of Danger)" by Tokyo Police Club *(Champ)*
"Hurricane" by Thirty Seconds to Mars *(This Is War)*
"Rocky Road To Dublin" by Dropkick Murphy's *(Live on St. Patrick's Day)*
"Stompa" by Serena Ryder *(Harmony)*
"Blue Jeans" by Lana Del Rey *(Born to Die)*
"Samba Pa Ti" by Tadeusz Machalski, self-released *(Guitar Collection)*
"Do I Wanna Know?" by Arctic Monkeys *(AM)*
"Sweater Weather" by The Neighbourhood *(I Love You)*
"Closer" by Nine Inch Nails *(The Downward Spiral)*
"Catch and Release" by Silversun Pickups *(Swoon)*
"Hips Don't Lie" by Shakira *(Oral Fixation, Vol. 2)*
"Desire" by Meg Myers *(Make a Shadow)*
"BTSK" by MS MR *(Secondhand Rapture)*
"Seven Devils" by Florence + The Machine *(Ceremonials)*
"Breathe" by Of Verona *(The White Apple)*
"Sanya Seiran" by Riley Kelly Lee *(Shakuhachi Honkyoku - Japanese Flute)*

"Howlin' For You" by The Black Keys *(Brothers)*
"Beauty of Sadness" by Spiky *(Whimsical Fantasy)*
"Silence" by Delerium (feat. Sarah McLachlan), DJ Tiësto
*(The Best of Delerium)*
"Breathing Underwater" by Metric *(Synthetica)*

# STEPPING STONE PLAYLIST

## Listen to it on Spotify!

"The Gates" by Young Empires *(The Gates)*
"That's Life" by Frank Sinatra *(Nothing But The Best)*
"Unsteady" by X Ambassadors *(VHS)*
"Smoke and Mirrors" by Imagine Dragons *(Smoke + Mirrors)*
"Ex's & Oh's" by Elle King *(Love Stuff)*
"Still Breathing" by Green Day *(Revolution Radio)*
"Erotica" by Madonna *(Erotica)*
"You and I" by PVARIS *(White Noise)*
"Until We Go Down" by Ruelle *(Up in Flames)*
"Numb" by Linkin Park *(Meteora)*
Mozart: Symphony No. 41 'Jupiter' by London Philharmonic Orchestra & Alfred Scholz *(111 Classical Masterpieces)*
"Alone" by Patricia Kaas *(Kabaret)*
"Dream a Little Dream of Me" by Ella Fitzgerald and Louis Armstrong *(Ella & Louis for Lovers)*

"Fever" by Peggy Lee *(The Best of Peggy Lee)*
"Wicked Game" by Ursine Vulpine feat. Annaca *(Single)*
"Save You" by Turin Breaks *(Lost Property)*
"Hallelujah" by Pentatonix *(A Pentatonix Christmas)*

# SET IN STONE PLAYLIST

## Listen to it on Spotify!

"Walk" by Foo Fighters *(Wasting Light)*
"The Way I Do" by Bishop Briggs *(The Way I Do - Single)*
"Blame" by Bastille *(Wild World)*
"Alive" by Sia *(This Is Acting)*
"La Vie En Rose" by Louis Armstrong *(Louis Armstrong's All-Time Greatest Hits)*
"So Cold" by Breaking Benjamin *(We Are Not Alone)*
"Drive" by Glades *(Drive - Single)*
"Falling Short" by Lapsley *(Understdy - EP)*
"Listen" by Claire Guerreso *(Listen - Single)*
"Roadside" by Rise Against *(The Sufferer & The Witness)*
"Chained to the Rhythm" by Katy Perry feat. Skip Marley *(Chained to the Rhythm)*
"Shape of You" by Ed Sheeran *(Ed Sheeran - ÷ Deluxe)*
"Can't Help Falling in Love" by Haley Reinhart *(Can't Help Falling In Love - Single)*
"Feeling Good" by Muse *(Origin of Symmetry)*
"Firestone" by Kygo feat. Conrad Sewell *(Cloud Nine)*

# WISHING STONE PLAYLIST

**To listen to Krystina's complete Christmas Playlist of more than 60 songs, check out the *Wishing Stone* song list on Spotify!**

*Baby, It's Cold Outside* by Dean Martin
*It's Beginning to Look a Lot Like Christmas* by Michael Bublé
*Song for a Winter's Night* by Sarah McLachlan
*Winter Sound* by Of Monsters and Men
*That's Christmas To Me* by Pentatonix
*Ave Maria* by Tadeusz Machalski
*Run Rudoloph Run* by Chuck Berry
*Merry Christmas Baby* by Bruce Springsteen & The E
Street Band
*Have Yourself a Merry Little Christmas* by Judy Garland
*Silver Bells* by Tony Bennett
*Twelve Days of Christmas* by Straight No Chaser

# BREAKING STONE PLAYLIST

## Listen to it on Spotify!

"Possession" by Sarah McLachlan
"In the End" Mellen Gi Remix by Tommee Profitt, Fleurie,
and Mellen Gi
"I Dare You" by Kelly Clarkson
"Gold on the Ceiling" by The Black KeyS
"Easy On Me" by Adele
"Hearts on Fire" by ILLENIUM, Dabin, Lights
"Play with Fire" by Sam Tinnesz (feat. Yacht Money)
"Don't Blame Me" by Taylor Swift
"Iris" by Natalie Taylor
"Falling" by Harry Styles
"Somewhere Over The Rainbow" by Israel
Kamakawiwo'ole
"White Flag" by Bishop BriggS
"Summer Wind" by Frank Sinatra
"In the Air Tonight" by Natalie Taylor
"War of Hearts" by Ruelle
"On An Evening In Roma" by Dean Martin
"Hold On: by Chord Overstreet

"I Know What You Want" by Busta Rhymes & Mariah Carey (feat. Flipmode Squad)
"Reckoning" by Alanis Morrissette
"What a Wonderful World" by Kina Grannis & Imaginary Future

# RECIPES

# MATTEO'S SPECIALTY DISHES

From the Specialty Menu
at Krystina's Place Restaurant

---

INSALATA CAPRESE
ANTIPASTO ITALIANO
EGGPLANT PARMIGIANA

# INSALATA CAPRESE
*(Caprese Salad)*

## Ingredients:

2 cups balsamic vinegar
3 ripe tomatoes
12 ounces fresh mozzarella, thickly sliced
Large bunch fresh basil leaves
Olive oil, for drizzling
Large pinch kosher salt
Large pinch freshly ground black pepper

## Directions:

Measure the balsamic vinegar and pour into a saucepan. Bring it to a gentle boil over a low heat. Cook it until the balsamic vinegar has reduced to a nice thick glaze (but still pourable), about 15 minutes. Oh and one other thing, your house will stink. But it's a good kind of stink, it's a vinegary stink. Allow the reduction to cool to room temperature before you serve it.

When you are ready to assemble the salad, cut the tomatoes into thick slices. Arrange them on a platter, alternating them with the mozzarella slices. Tuck the whole basil leaves in between the tomato and cheese slices.

Drizzle on the gorgeous, almost black balsamic reduction.

Then drizzle olive oil in a thin stream over the top. Finally, sprinkle on salt and pepper.

# ANTIPASTO ITALIANO
*(Italian Antipasta)*

**Ingredients:**
8 oz Italian assorted meats: prosciutto, Calabrese Salami,
Capocollo, Bresaola
6 oz smoked wild salmon
8 oz mozzarella di Buffala (drained)
16 sticks grissini (bread sticks)
1 large heirloom tomato
6 oz marinated artichoke hearts (drained)
5 oz Sicilian Olives (or your favorite mix)
5 oz pepperoncini (drained)
5 oz oz roasted peppers (drained)
6 oz cherry peppers (drained)
1/4 c fresh basil leaves
1/2 tspq red pepper flakes

*Basic Crostini*
8 slices baguette
1 clove garlic
1/4 c extra virgin olive oil

*Roasted Pepper Olive Tapenade*
8 oz roasted peppers (drained)
6 oz olives (drained)
1 tbsp red wine vinegar
3 cloves garlic (grated)
3 tbsp extra virgin olive oil + more if needed

*Whipped Goat Cheese*
6 oz goat cheese
4 tbsp extra virgin olive oil
1/4 c fresh chives

*Whipped Ricotta*
1 c ricotta cheese
1 lug olive oil
Zest from 1 lemon
1 pinch sea salt

## Instructions:
*Crostini*
Preheat a cast iron griddle and grill the sliced baguette until nice char marks form. Gently rub each one with a garlic clove and brush lightly with olive oil. Set on the board.

*Tapenade*
To make the tapenade process the olives with the roasted red peppers, garlic, olive oil and red wine vinegar in a food processor until a rustic texture forms. Adjust seasonings with some sea salt and transfer to a small serving bowl.

*Whipped Goat Cheese*
Add the goat cheese olive oil and fresh chives to the bowl of a mini food processor and puree for a couple of minutes until whipped. Using a small spoon stuff cherry peppers with some of the whipped goat cheese. Transfer what's left

to a bowl, cover with plastic wrap and refrigerate together with the peppers until ready to plate.

*Whipped Ricotta*
Transfer the ricotta cheese with a lug of olive oil and lemon zest to a food processor and process until fluffy and smooth, about a minute or so.

*Plate your Antipasto*
Place your serving platter on top of a large cheese board. Start with the olive tapenade bowl, followed by the marinated olives in a small bowl, surrounded by the roasted peppers, pepperoncini and artichoke hearts.

Spoon dollops of whipped ricotta and whipped goat cheese in between. Gently start tucking slices of the salami, prosciutto and smoked salmon all throughout.

Slice the mozzarella and tomatoes and layer them with basil slices. Place them on the board continuing the spread away from the main plate.

Use some of the prosciutto slices to wrap around the grissini and place on the platter.

Finish the entire spread with a light drizzle of good extra virgin olive oil, a pinch of course sea salt and red pepper flakes. Garnish with more fresh basil.

# EGGPLANT PARMIGIANA

## Ingredients:

### MARINARA
¼ cup olive oil
1 head of garlic, cloves crushed
1 large red onion, chopped
3 oil-packed anchovy fillets (optional)
½ teaspoon crushed red pepper flakes
1 Tbsp. tomato paste
¼ cup dry white wine
2 - 28-oz. cans whole peeled tomatoes
¼ cup torn basil leaves
½ tsp. dried oregano
Kosher salt

### EGGPLANT
4 pounds Italian eggplants (about 4 medium eggplants),
peeled, sliced lengthwise ½–¾ inch thick
Kosher salt
3 cups panko breadcrumbs
1½ tsp. dried oregano
1 tsp. freshly ground black pepper
1½ cups finely grated Parmesan, divided
1½ cups all-purpose flour
5 large eggs, beaten to blend
1⅓ cups olive oil
½ cup finely chopped basil and parsley, plus basil leaves
for serving

6 ounces low-moisture mozzarella, grated (about 1⅓ cups)
8 ounces fresh mozzarella, thinly sliced

## Preparation:

## MARINARA

Step 1
Preheat oven to 350°. Place a Dutch oven or other large heavy ovenproof pot over medium heat. Add oil and garlic and cook, stirring often, until garlic is golden, about 4 minutes. Add onion, anchovies (if using), and red pepper flakes and cook, stirring often, until onion is translucent, about 5 minutes. Stir in tomato paste and cook, stirring often, until slightly darkened, about 2 minutes. Add wine, bring to a boil, and cook until almost completely evaporated, about 1 minute. Add tomatoes, breaking up with your hands, and their juices; add basil and oregano and stir to combine. Swirl 1½ cups water into one tomato can, then the other, to rinse, and add to pot; season with salt. Transfer pot to oven; roast sauce, stirring halfway through, until thick and tomatoes are browned on top and around edges of pot, 2–2½ hours.

Step 2
Let sauce cool slightly. Pass through the large holes of a food mill or process in a food processor until mostly smooth. Taste and season with salt.
Do Ahead: Sauce can be made 2 days ahead. Cover and chill.

## EGGPLANT

### Step 3
Lightly season eggplant slices all over with salt; place in a single layer on several layers of paper towels inside a rimmed baking sheet. Top with another layer of paper towels and more slices; repeat as needed. Top with a final layer of paper towels, then another rimmed baking sheet; weigh down with a heavy pot. Let eggplant sit until it has released excess liquid, 45–60 minutes. This step gives the eggplant a creamy texture when baked.

### Step 4
Meanwhile, pulse panko, oregano, pepper, and ¾ cup Parmesan in a food processor until very finely ground. Transfer to a shallow bowl.

### Step 5
Preheat oven to 350°. Place flour in another shallow bowl and eggs in a third shallow bowl. Working one at a time, dredge eggplant slices in flour, then dip in egg, allowing excess to drip off. Coat in breadcrumbs, packing all around, then shaking off excess. Place on wire racks.

### Step 6
Heat ⅔ cup oil in a large skillet, preferably cast iron, over medium-high. Cook as many eggplant slices as will comfortably fit in pan, turning once, until deep golden, about 5 minutes. Transfer to paper towels and immediately press with more paper towel to absorb oil. Working in batches, repeat with remaining eggplant, adding

remaining ⅔ cup oil and wiping out skillet as needed. Let cool. Taste and season with more salt if needed.

Step 7

Toss chopped herbs, low-moisture mozzarella, and remaining ¾ cup Parmesan in a medium bowl. Spread 1 cup sauce over the bottom of a 13x9" baking pan; top with a layer of eggplant slices (trim as needed). Drizzle 1 cup sauce over and sprinkle with one-third of cheese mixture. Add another layer of eggplant, followed by 1 cup sauce and half of remaining cheese mixture. Repeat layers with remaining slices, sauce, and cheese mixture. Cover with foil and bake on a rimmed baking sheet until eggplant is custardy, 45–60 minutes.

Step 8

Remove from oven and arrange fresh mozzarella over eggplant. Increase oven temperature to 425° and bake, uncovered, until cheese is bubbling and browned in spots, 15–20 minutes longer. Let rest 30 minutes. Top with basil leaves just before slicing.

# VIVIAN'S HOLIDAY COOKIES

CUCCIDATI
KRIS KRINGLE CUT-OUT COOKIES
MOLASSES COOKIES

# CUCCIDATI
### *(Italian Fig Cookies)*

## Ingredients:
*Dough*
3 eggs
¼ tsp. vanilla
¼ tsp. milk
¾ cup sugar
6 Tbsp. Shortening
Dash of salt
1 Tbsp. baking powder
4 cups flour

*Filling*
12 oz. figs
8 oz. dates
4 oz. raisins
½ cup walnuts
1 orange with skins
¼ cup brown sugar
¼ cup white sugar
¼ tsp. cinnamon
1/8 cup strawberry preserves

## Directions:
Preheat oven to 375°.  Cream shortening.  Add sugar, eggs, and milk.  Mix well.  Add dry ingredients and mix until dough can be rolled.  Set dough aside and make filling. Grind and mix all ingredients for filling.  Set aside.

Roll out dough and cut into 3 inch squares.  Place a small amount of filling on each square.  Seal two corners together.  (Alternative: To save time, roll a long strip and place filling along the center. Roll into a long tube and cut at an angle.)

Bake for 10-12 minutes.  Frost when cool and sprinkle with colored sugar.

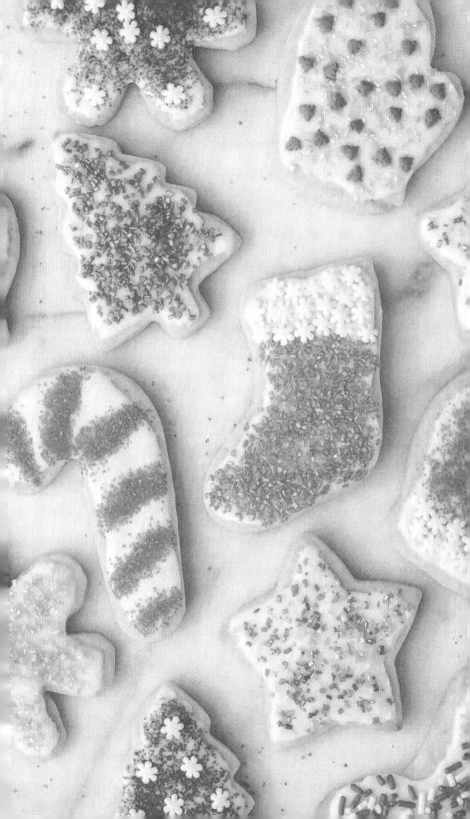

# KRIS KRINGLE CUT-OUT COOKIES

## Ingredients:
1 cup butter
2 cups sugar
1 tsp. vanilla
3 eggs
1 ½ tsp. cream of tartar
1 ½ tsp. baking soda, dissolved in 2 Tbsp. milk
1 tsp. salt
4 ½ cups flour

## Directions:
Mix all ingredients, except flour. Mix well. Add 3 cups of flour. Add additional flour to make a dough that can be rolled. Roll dough. Using cookie cutters, create your shapes of choice. Bake at 400° on an ungreased cookie sheet for 8 – 15 minutes, depending on thickness. Decorate when cooled.

# MOLASSES COOKIES

## Ingredients:

¾ cups shortening
1 cup sugar
¼ cup molasses
1 egg
2 tsp. baking soda
2 cups flour
½ tsp. cloves
½ tsp. ginger
1 tsp. cinnamon
½ tsp. salt

## Directions:

Melt shortening in a saucepan and then allow to cool. Add sugar, molasses, and egg. Beat well. Sift dry ingredients. Add to molasses mixture and mix well. Chill in refrigerator for at least 2 hours.

Preheat oven to 375°. Form dough into 1″ balls. Roll in granulated sugar. Place two inches apart on a greased cookie sheet. Bake for 8 – 10 minutes.

## ABOUT THE AUTHOR

 Dakota Willink is an award-winning USA Today Bestselling Author from New York. She loves writing about damaged heroes who fall in love with sassy and independent females. Her books are character-driven, emotional, and sexy, yet written with a flare that keeps them real. With a wide range of publications, Dakota's imagination is constantly spinning new ideas. Her work has been translated into five languages and she has sold over 1 million books worldwide.

Dakota often says she survived her first publishing with coffee and wine. She's an unabashed *Star Wars* fanatic and still dreams of getting her letter from Hogwarts one day. Her daily routines usually include rocking Lululemon yoga pants, putting on lipstick, and obsessing over Excel spreadsheets. Two spoiled Cavaliers are her furry writing companions who bring her regular smiles. She enjoys traveling with her husband and debating social and economic issues with her politically savvy Generation Z son and daughter.

Dakota's favorite book genres include contemporary or dark romance, political & psychological thrillers, and autobiographies.

## AWARDS, ACCOLADES, AND OTHER PROJECTS

*The Stone Series* is Dakota's first published book series. It has been recognized for various awards and bestseller lists, including *USA Today* and the *Readers' Favorite* 2017 Gold Medal in Romance, and has since been translated into multiple languages internationally.

The *Fade Into You* series (formally known as the *Cadence* duet) was a finalist in the *HEAR Now Festival Independent Audiobook Awards*.

In addition, Dakota has written under the alternate pen name, Marie Christy. Under this name, she has written and published a children's book for charity titled, *And I Smile*.

Also writing as Marie Christy, she was a contributor to the Blunder Woman Productions project, *Nevertheless We Persisted: Me Too*, a 2019 *Audie Award Finalist* and *Earphones Awards Winner*. This project inspired Dakota to write *The Sound of Silence*, a dark romantic suspense novel that tackles the realities of domestic abuse.

Dakota Willink is the founder of Dragonfly Ink Publishing, whose mission is to promote a common passion for reading by partnering with like-minded authors and industry professionals. Through this company, Dakota created the *Love & Lace Inkorporated* Magazine and the *Leave Me Breathless World*, hosted ALLURE Audiobook Con, and sponsored various charity anthologies.

## OFFICIAL WEBSITE
www.dakotawillink.com

---

## SUBSCRIBE TO DAKOTA'S NEWSLETTER
My newsletter goes out once a week. It's packed with new content, sales on signed paperbacks and Angel Book Boxes from my online store, and giveaways. Don't miss out!

I value your email address and promise to NEVER spam you. SUBSCRIBE HERE: https://dakotawillink.com/subscribe

## BOOKS & BOXED WINE CONFESSIONS

Want fun stuff and sneak peek excerpts from Dakota? Join Books & Boxed Wine Confessions and get the inside scoop! Fans in this interactive reader Facebook group are the first to know the latest news!

JOIN HERE: https://www.facebook.com/groups/1635080436793794